Now That You're Rich

Let's Fall in Love!

DURJOY DATTA

MAANVI AHUJA

Penguin
metro reads

PENGUIN METRO READS

Published by the Penguin Group

Penguin Books India Pvt. Ltd, 11 Community Centre, Panchsheel Park, New Delhi 110 017, India

Penguin Group (USA) Inc., 375 Hudson Street, New York, New York 10014, USA

Penguin Group (Canada), 90 Eglinton Avenue East, Suite 700, Toronto, Ontario, M4P 2Y3, Canada (a division of Pearson Penguin Canada Inc.)

Penguin Books Ltd, 80 Strand, London WC2R 0RL, England

Penguin Ireland, 25 St Stephen's Green, Dublin 2, Ireland (a division of Penguin Books Ltd)

Penguin Group (Australia), 707 Collins Street, Melbourne, Victoria 3008, Australia (a division of Pearson Australia Group Pty Ltd)

Penguin Group (NZ), 67 Apollo Drive, Rosedale, Auckland 0632, New Zealand (a division of Pearson New Zealand Ltd)

Penguin Books (South Africa) (Pty) Ltd, Block D, Rosebank Office Park, 181 Jan Smuts Avenue, Parktown North, Johannesburg 2193, South Africa

Penguin Books Ltd, Registered Offices: 80 Strand, London WC2R 0RL, England

First published by Grapevine India Publishers 2011
Published in Penguin Metro Reads by Penguin Books India 2013

Copyright © Durjoy Datta 2013

ISBN 9780143421610

Typeset in Adobe Caslon Pro by Eleven Arts, Delhi
Printed at Manipal Technologies Ltd, Manipal

To Shelly (1998–2009)
The bravest, cutest and smartest dog ever. We will miss you.

You Need to Hear This

I have always been terrible with secrets and stories that are never meant to be told or passed on. A very feminine trait, I know. But then, stories are meant to be told, aren't they?

Lazing in my cosy couch today, with a laptop on my lap, I can't help but recall a story that I have told a million times, no matter how many times I have been asked to shut up.

But I find no reasons as to why I shouldn't pen this one down and entertain a few souls while irritating a few others. What the heck! I will write it.

This one, I think, has all the elements: a guy with a Porsche, a girl lost in love, selfish parents, loving siblings, a love scene on a thirteenth-floor terrace, lecherous seniors, blackmail, life-altering videos, hideous bosses, infinitely sexy co-workers, drunk guys professing undying love and last but not the least . . . definitely not the least . . . *money*.

Fifty years after you get married, you find women with no grey hair desirable, you find women who are not obese attractive; whoever that woman might be, she won't be your wife. The girl you're in love with today, the girl who you think is smart and interesting and pretty, will be the one who will make you feel your skull is being clawed open with Wolverine paws. Love is often blind, and it blinds you short-term and makes you overlook what time changes.

Love makes the world go round. But money buys the tickets.

Maybe, love lasts a lifetime. Money lasts longer. It pays for the funeral, too.

Falling in love is easy. Choose the sweet guy who sits next to you in class and flutter your eyelashes at him, or pick the girl who does as much as talk to you, exchange numbers, be her wake-up call in the morning, send sweet text messages telling him or her how much they meant to you, and BAM! You are in Love.

So, what's wrong?

The analysis . . . You forget to analyse how this situation will play out after a decade when the girl or the guy is no longer pretty and they are predictable and boring. You forget to ask yourself the simplest and the most obvious of questions.

Is the guy rich? Is the girl rich? Does the girl have a brother? Am I ready to be with him after thirty years, come what may? Will I be happy with a husband who has not been to the gym since his teens when he used to be buff and fit, and is now fat and lazy? Will he be able to sustain my needs and the kids who are going to wreak havoc later?

Will I be happy after ten years with the girl who now dresses up like someone's dead? Will I be happy to see her wrinkled smile twenty years down the line, with bills piling up at my doorstep?

Will I tolerate it with a smile when she tells me that the neighbour just bought a new car and she wishes to have one, too?

One answer settles it all.

Marry rich, very rich.

We are nice people, and for us, relationships are meant to last a lifetime. If they don't, the guy is a bastard and a jerk, and the girl is a cheating slut. So, till the time that changes, choose your date for tonight carefully. You might just end up spending a lifetime together.

Fall in love carefully. Piles and wads of money usually break the fall and make for a smoother landing. So, now that the pearls of wisdom have trickled down my brain to the recesses of yours, let us go on with the story.

It's the story of the four of them.

Overachievers. Geeks. Nerds. The ones who ask for sheets after sheets in examination halls while you look blankly at the question paper, cursing yourself for not studying the night before. The ones will be out with the answer while you are still looking for your calculator, trying to figure out which numbers to tap. Whom would you not consider as serious contenders while predicting class ranks? Olympiad winners? College gold medallists?

All four of them, brilliant minds.

The first amongst them, Abhijeet, exemplified everything I just said. He had yet to score in the eighties, or the seventies; anything less than the mid-nineties depressed him and for good reaon. He was the most hardworking student you would ever come across.

He had led an uneventful life. The craziest thing he had ever done was to take an exam with a chapter not revised. So, let me start from the day he spent his last day as a college topper, when something remotely *happening* happened.

1

It was the fourth of January and the air in the college campus was redolent with expectations and the sweat of his fellow classmates who were still looking for jobs.

There were more than a few pairs of eyes on him; most of them had disgust dripping from them. A few greeted him and the others looked away. He had already been placed in a company which offered him seventeen lakhs per annum, but he wanted more. The company on campus that day was offering thirty lakh Indian rupees per annum. It was an opportunity of a lifetime.

He left the presentation that the Human Resources of the company had prepared especially for the students of Shri Ram College of Commerce and headed for the library where he came across a few of his professors. They wished him luck and said they had full faith in his capabilities. Abhijeet was too brilliant for his own good. He was good enough to be hated.

I need this. This is what I want to do, he told himself and trudged to the library. He passed the college bookshop and spotted a few of his classmates in an intense discussion with Raju bhaiya. Raju had seen hundreds of students spend the best three years of their lives in front of him. Years later, they would discuss him in their reunions, but Abhijeet would never be a part of those discussions because he had been too busy with books and seniors and sucking up to his professors. Being the brilliant college topper for two years in a row was a full-time job that hardly left any time for friends or frolic.

Macroeconomics, by Ravi Shastri. He flipped through the pages. There was nothing new. He flipped through some other books. Accounts. Business Studies. Law.

Same thing.

The last two years of spending hours neck-deep in those books, while others were looking down cleavages, held him in good stead.

Abhijeet had been brought up in a single income family. His father worked in the Delhi Development Authority while his mother was a housewife. The glaring difference between his father and his uncles' wealth always pinched him: their cars, their big houses and the big rings on their fingers. He always felt he was missing out on something. Though his parents did whatever they could for him, he did not like it when his uncle discussed business and laughed out loud at losses that were more than his father's yearly income. He wanted to make it big. This was his day and his chance to get back at them. While his cousins were waiting in the wings to join their fathers in their dingy manufacturing units that made plastic buckets and trinkets, it was his chance to become a front-end investment banker, the most grossly overpaid and overworked of all white collar jobs.

Abhijeet was always conspicuous by his presence. He was a Delhi Board 2004 topper, an NTSE scholar and CA foundation rank one. Everybody knew who he was. Some girls even found him cute, but then, girls also say that about stray puppies. Big deal.

But I wouldn't really call him average-looking with his just-right complexion, lean frame and chocolate-boy looks on a six-foot frame. He was better-looking than many guys around, but he hid behind huge rimmed glasses, dull shirts and oversized trousers. The worn-out white sport shoes under the loose dirt-brown trousers just made things worse.

That morning, it had been hardly a few minutes since he had started reading an article on subprime losses and their fallout when he heard a meek, squeaky voice of a girl.

Riya had just joined college and looked so. She stood no taller than Abhijeet's shoulder and had a baby face that had not left her since eighth standard. She was *as* fair and *as* cute as they get. Beyond measure. Nice baby-like eyes. Small pouty pink lips. The brightest shade of pink could be named after her. A big smile was her biggest asset; it never left her face.

Abhijeet was used to juniors coming to him with questions about professors, subjects and career options. For the juniors looking to emulate Abhijeet in academics, he was a helpful senior and an eager guide.

She pulled up a chair, and after congratulating him for his placement with HLL, the conversation shifted to other things.

'But all my friends are taking tuitions,' she said and her lips curved downwards when Abhijeet dismissed tuition centres for being money-sucking business ventures with no commitment towards results or academic excellence.

'If you concentrate hard enough in the classes and don't miss any, I don't think you need to spend so much on tuitions.'

'Yes, I guess. But you are a topper. It's easy for you to say this.'

'It's not that. Attend classes and you too will do well. It's easy.'

'But who will attend all the classes?' she asked and leaned back on her chair. A little shorter and her feet would not have touched the floor. 'There is so much to do. There is the choreography team, the Western dance team . . . there are so many movies to watch . . . the new one . . . Johnny Depp is looking so hot in it, even though I don't like his beard . . . but that is okay . . . and there is this nice new party place near Vasant Kunj, you've got to go there . . . you just can't miss it. It is done in pink and blue . . . it is wonderful . . . and add to that, shopping and old friends from school and new friends from college . . . there is no time left . . . Oh! And there is a new Bercos in Kamla Nagar and it is so *eww* . . . but there is this small shop near it which has these real nice earrings . . .'

She went on and on and on. Abhijeet did not mind, he was busy noticing her. Her white T-shirt hung down from a shoulder and showed a strap—pink.

Her T-shirt spelled out *Sugar*—in pink. There was *perfect* colour harmony. Earrings and shoes. Shoes and bangles. Bangles and hair colour. There were about twenty shades of pink on her that day. She even smelled pink.

'Riya?' somebody shouted from behind them.

'Oh . . . I must get going. We are going for a movie today. Thank you, sir.'

'Missing classes again?'

'Yes,' she crinkled her nose and smiled. 'Bye,' she said, clutched her bright pink handbag and left.

He followed the skin-fit jeans with little fake diamonds on them and the screaming pink handbag, as she hopped across the library and joined her friends. For a girl of her height, she had considerable curves, almost like a miniature Beyoncé. She would grow up to be a voluptuous and attractive woman, that is, if she ever grew up.

Abhijeet smiled at himself and got back to his newspaper, running the conversation over and over again in his mind, reliving it again. Blood had rushed from every vein to his face and his cheeks had turned into a shade of red.

This day defined his life.

Not only did he have the single longest conversation with a girl, he was through Silverman Finance and was officially on his way to be an investment banker in a few months' time.

~

Geeks fall in love way too quickly. It's for the simple reason that it is not every day that a girl so cute comes up to them and starts a conversation.

Abhijeet was in *love*. Deep true, eternal, undying love!

It was his third plate of Maggi and his stomach was about to revolt, but he could not think of a better reason to sit outside her class, which faced the canteen.

The hour changed. The class changed . . . but there was no sign of her.

The last three days of waiting finally yielded a positive result as she walked past him, surrounded by friends, hopping between them and screeching at the top of her voice as she begged them to miss another class and go bowling. Abhijeet sat up and prayed that she would notice him.

She and another classmate of hers stayed back while the others entered the class.

Abhijeet alternated between staring at his plate and looking at her, keeping a page half turned to look busy. She was in the same colours as she had been the other day. She wore a baby pink T-shirt that hung loosely over her and seemed to have been picked out from the kids' section of a garment store. The sun reflected off her face and it glowed bright yellow. Her long straight-pressed hair that came down to her waist was shining.

She did not see him.

He sat there, waiting for her to notice him, often changing positions, getting up and then sitting down again, rustling the pages in order to catch her attention, but nothing worked.

Disappointed, he got up to leave.

Just as he crossed her, she noticed him and came running over, her waving her handbag in the air, a different one but pink nevertheless.

'Hi! Where are you going?' she asked. 'Oh . . . by the way, congratulations for getting through! I told all my friends about you and they went nuts that I know the guy who got placed with Silverman Finance! Isn't that just the dream? But then I told them that we have just talked once and then they were like *okay* . . . but you've got to admit . . . I am your lucky charm. We talked and you got through, so I deserve a treat and I know this place and it's really nice . . . but you look so tired, what happened?'

Abhijeet had started blushing again.

'Nothing.'

'Okay, listen, I've got to go now because I have this practice . . . it's the Western dance thing and the competition is in two months and you have got to see it. Okay, got to go, catch you later, bye!'

'Okay, bye!'

She left him smiling ear-to-ear.

~

Gradually, Riya started noticing Abhijeet around all the time. Ignoring someone who's always where you are is usually quite tough and Abhijeet made sure he was always in sight of Riya.

Small conversations started to brew and they soon exchanged numbers. Abhijeet used to stare at the number for hours on an end.

Free time between classes was spent at the Café Coffee Day nearby. Messages were exchanged, day in and day out. Generally, if you are exchanging more than twenty messages with a girl in a day, I would say you are in *love* . . . or if you're not, you will be and will regret it when you get caught in the friend zone.

They were getting closer each passing day. Her innocent charm had him in knots every time she smiled at him and he helped her cope with the daily rigour of college.

'I really don't need this,' Abhijeet said to her as she held out a pair of jeans, faded near the crotch and the knees and the back pockets. She had taken him to accompany her on one of her shopping sprees, but seeing him in the mirror, so awfully dressed, she couldn't help herself.

'Are you crazy? This is what everyone is wearing these days! Seen OC? 90210? EVERYONE! You've just *got to* have one of these. Trust me, they'll look awesome. You have the face and the physique for it. Just go, try them. Next, we will try those ones there, they are a little expensive but you can't miss out on those,' she said, as she pushed him into the fitting room.

She got him two new pairs of jeans, some T-shirts and rimless spectacles and he looked great in them. She stood next to him, clutching his arm as he stood in front of the mirror, wearing a red T-shirt with an illegible graphic on it, a clinging pair of jeans, brand-new sneakers and a new pair of spectacles. He was unrecognizable. Riya kept pulling his jeans down, every time he tried to pull it up to his navel.

He admitted that it was the best he had ever looked.

~

There was not a time in the day when he wasn't thinking about her. Her face never left his eyes, her voice, his ears. He spent hours sitting and staring at blank walls, running their conversations through his head and recounting times they had spent together. He read her texts over and over again, he saw the grainy pictures they took together on their cell phones, and wondered if he could go back to that time.

He had lost consciousness of time and space and was with her, every moment, every second of the day. He'd never felt this good in all his short, studious life. He felt nice about himself, he felt loved. Her face was the most beautiful thing in the world for him. Those eyes, those lips, that smile.

Months passed and they became the thickest of friends. Abhijeet was the first person who was told everything: screwed class tests, a bitching friend, new shoes at Puma, stringy tops at Kazo, unfair parents, horrible guys in Delhi transport buses. Everything.

First love is always tricky. It promises a lot, but more often than not, it is just a practice ground for subsequent relationships. To Abhijeet, it did a world of good, for he changed from a raging nerd to a cute *guy-next-door* in a matter of days. Cool tees, chappals, random accessories et al. His oiled hair now got a rough grunge cut, falling over his eyebrows. And finally, his tongue didn't end up in knots while talking to a girl. He was a different guy now, but what had not changed was his love for her.

As more time passed, Abhijeet had no doubt in his mind that she was as much in love with him as he was with her and we can't blame him for that. He was too stupid to see anything, too stupid to see Riya walking away from him whenever her phone beeped, too stupid to see her smiling stupidly when she received a text. Riya never felt the need to tell him about Arjun. *Girls* usually never do and tend to miss out on details that matter most to the guys around them. *Guys* are expected to understand, but they, too, never do.

What are you doing tonight? *Does she mean she wants to have sex with me?* Do you live alone? *Does she mean she wants to come over?* Do you have a girlfriend? *Does she mean she wants to be mine?* What girls mean by these sentences, no one has the slightest idea.

However, Abhijeet was in for a rude shock that day at the choreography competition in which Riya was participating. She had handed over her cell phone to Abhijeet just before she went backstage to change for her performance. After a while, the cell phone started ringing.

Sweetheart calling . . .

Abhijeet's mind went blank for a few seconds. He dismissed it, thinking it must be a female friend of hers. The call was not answered. And then six more calls went unanswered.

Abhijeet, with trembling hands, looked at the number and it looked familiar. He noticed that only the last digit was different from Riya's. He had *heard* of many couples who buy those numbers because of cheap calling rates, end up talking throughout the night, get bored, fight, and eventually break up. Ideally, couples should get the most expensive calling plan and keep the mystery alive . . . let a year pass by before you know your girl has a dog.

He checked the inbox, as Riya came on stage wearing glittery clothes.

Every second text in her inbox was from the same number.

Hi. Where are you? Miss you. See you soon.
Best of luck, sweetheart. Might get a little late. Sorry. Love.
  Muah.
I love you. You are the best thing that ever happened to me.
  Lots of slurpies. Muah.

Abhijeet looked at her dancing and noticed a distant, indifferent look in her eyes. He re-read the messages and checked the call details. It was obvious who *Sweetheart* was, and he was crushed. He resisted the urge to throw the phone away. He clenched his fists and hoped he had not checked her phone. Abhijeet looked for somebody from her batch and handed over her things to him, and tried to fight the tears.

He wanted to leave that very moment but waited till the end of her performance.

He waited till she came back from the changing room, her eyes still laced with mascara and glitter, and she was still looking for somebody. The very next second, a smart, nice-looking guy appeared and hugged her. The embrace was more than just a friendly hug, and the tears he'd tried to hold back, rolled down Abhijeet's cheeks.

Abhijeet spent the next two hours walking around aimlessly on the streets of Delhi University, wishing things were different, wishing he had not checked her phone, wishing he had never met her. He checked the call timings of every single call and read every single message. He read the tissue paper she had once given him after writing something on it, and threw it away. Only to pick it up again, uncrumple it and keep it safe. He could still see her smiling right in front of him. He realized he had not asked her to love him. It wasn't her fault, but it wasn't his fault either. He wiped his tears and slowly walked back home. Smiling, as he saw her smiling. Right in front of him.

He texted her: *Your performance was great.*

～

After a few days of staying out of Riya's sight, she caught hold of him while he was entering the class.

'Abhijeet?' she called out.

He looked back to see her running towards him. He had been dying to see her.

'Yes.'

'Can we talk? Unless you have something to do? Please, I have something to tell you. And why did you leave that day? Can we go to the Café Coffee Day? It has this new fat-free coffee and it is fabulous and we just *have to* go . . .'

'I have a class to attend and I don't want to miss it.'

'But you can miss the class! I have so much to talk to you about.'

'No, I can't miss the class.'

Abhijeet snubbed her and entered the classroom.

After a few minutes of macroeconomics, he walked out of the class and ran in the direction Riya had gone. She was sitting on the pavement, polishing her nails, but the glint in her eyes was missing.

'Hey.'

'So, you decided to miss the class?'

'Yeah.'

'You can attend it if you want to, but the coffee is real nice. Let my nails dry out first. This is a new one, my mom's friend got it from the States and it's teak pink. Really nice, no?'

'You wanted to talk about something,' Abhijeet said irritably.

'Yes, are you pissed at me? You don't pick up my calls and don't even reply to my messages. And you went that day without even meeting me. I should be the one pissed at you.'

'Is this what you wanted to talk about?' he asked. His heart was aching to say that he loved her, and he felt cheated that she was in love with somebody else.

'No, it's about something else. Actually, it's about Arjun. That guy, uff, doesn't even know how to eat with a fork and he makes me wait for so long! And that day, he wore a green checked shirt and that, too, in front of my friends. I mean who wears that? I mean, he is so tacky and acts like he is the coolest guy ever . . .'

'What is your point, Riya?'

'He stood me up again.'

'That can happen sometimes,' he said, wondering why, why after all this while did she finally decide to mention Arjun in front of him. He had heard the name before from her, but he was never talked about as a boyfriend.

'Are you kidding me? I was there standing in the heat for two hours. I was out of sunscreen and he didn't come. What's worse, his phone was switched off.' Riya stopped talking. She had tears in her eyes.

'What happened?' Abhijeet said, now paying attention.

'It is just that I think he doesn't love me any more. It has been so long since he got me something nice, and we don't meet that often any more. I mean, I cancelled my shopping date for a date with him and he simply doesn't care. He just cares about his friends and takes me for granted. And that friend of his, the one whom I told you about, *arey,* the girl who wears tacky platform heels . . .' The tears had started peeking out. 'I love him, Abhijeet, and I don't know what is happening to him.'

'Everything will be fine,' Abhijeet said half-heartedly.

'I hope so. And I hope he stops wearing those cargos he bought like a year ago.' The tears were still trickling down.

Just as Abhijeet was about to put his hand on her head, he saw the familiar face walking in their direction, the face from the choreography competition.

'I think your boyfriend is coming.'

She looked up and immediately started wiping away her tears. She took out a handkerchief and rubbed it all across her face, trying to remove all traces of the weeping bout.

'Do I look okay?'

'Yes.'

'Are my eyes red?'

'A little bit.'

'Does it look like I was crying?'

'Not really.'

'The mascara?'

'Looks fine.'

'The cheeks?'

'Pink.'

'We are . . .'

'Best friends,' Abhijeet said. Riya had taught him this.

Abhijeet watched them leave, with Arjun trying to put an arm across to pull her close.

Abhijeet suddenly remembered every time Riya had mentioned Arjun's name in front of him. Arjun used to drop her to college sometimes. He had a big car, Honda or something. Not that he was very good-looking, but everything he wore was expensive. Somewhere deep inside, he felt he wasn't worthy of Riya. He wasn't as swanky or rich as Arjun was. It had started pinching him. Arjun's affluence only made him feel worse about his modest background; being middle class was his curse.

~

Arjun's behaviour towards Riya had been deteriorating by the day and she had been living in denial. Double denial. She knew she was being wronged. And she *knew* she was refusing to see it.

Riya's complaints about him had gone beyond mere missed dates, bad shoes and crumpled shirts. They had real problems now. Arjun had changed his relationship status to *single* on Facebook and was entertaining random girls. One question asked and Riya was shouted at for being nagging. It happened every day and Abhijeet often found her in tears.

His closeness to Riya had been double-edged for Abhijeet. For every time she said she had never had a friend like him, he felt privileged. Every time he chose a nail polish for her, he felt important. Every time he was the first person to see the new streaks in her hair, he felt complete. However, seeing her so madly in love with someone else, killed him. He wished her perfectly manicured hands were in his, not Arjun's.

Riya had noticed the change in Abhijeet's behaviour but she chose to ignore it. Crushes and first loves are hard to deal with.

~

'Will you please stop crying?' Abhijeet said for the seventh time that evening. Arjun was still being a jerk and it was taking a toll on Riya. Riya's condition had gone from bad to worse. She had started talking less.

That day was the first time he had seen her without her eye make-up. Not that she looked any less cute.

'Sorry.'

'You don't have to be.'

It was the same story every time. Arjun did something that she didn't think was right and she spent time crying over it in front

of Abhijeet till the time she ran out of tears and simply fo~~
what she was crying about.

'What happened?'

'Nothing.'

'I want to know. I can't see you like this. So quiet. You haven't even shopped for a week now. No new shoes. No bangles. Even your earrings don't match your shoes today and that's a problem!'

'Really?' She checked out her shoes and smiled behind those tears. 'Of course, they match! You are so mean.'

'So, now tell me what happened? You know you're going to tell me eventually.'

'He says I am boring.'

'As in?'

'As in, *physically*.' She kept crying. 'He is asking me to give in ... Sleep with him ...'

'*Is he insane?* What the ...! How can he ask you to do that?'

'He says every friend of his is doing it and he expects me ...'

'What did you do?'

'I can't, but I love him and despite everything, he is sweet ...'

'So what will you do?'

'I don't know. Maybe he is right. Even Kritika has done it with her boyfriend. So ... but ...'

'*So?*'

Every word of hers hit him like a boulder thrown right at his face. He knew in all probability that Riya would become physically involved with Arjun, but hearing it from her mouth made him burst into a million pieces inside, and that she would do it because he wanted it, filled him with unbridled rage. His eyes welled up and he looked away before she could notice them.

'Leave him,' he said and wiped his tears off.

'I can't.'

'What do you mean *you can't*? Of course you can! You are cute and smart and you can get any guy you want!'

'I can't, I love him, I love him so much. Just last week, he got me this real cute teddy bear key chain, said the sweetest things, and then we even went to that place. Oh no, that was you! Sorry, but I love him and I always will.'

'*You call this love? Haan?* You call this love? He is bloody abusing you. Can't you see that?' Abhijeet's voice started to rise and the tears returned to his eyes. He banged his fist on the table and started to breathe heavily.

'But . . .'

'What but! That bastard! All he wants is to fuck you. Are you really this blind?' He stood up and started moving around in circles, coming close to her and shouting at her. He wanted to grab her by the shoulders, shake her and wake her up.

'Abhijeet! Mind your language! He is my boyfriend and it's none of your business!'

'Mind your own business? What the hell? You know what my business is? I will show you what my business is, no, wait, I will show you what my business is.' He rummaged through his bag, throwing half of his things around, and took out three neatly done assignments.

'This is my business. This is economics.' He threw it in her lap. 'Microeconomics. And law. Last date tomorrow. You don't even know when these were given. Who did this? *I did.* It took me all night. I did it. Not that bastard. I love you. I am the one who has been in love with you for the last six months. Not him. I am the one who is listening to you and seeing you cry every day. Not him. And what do you do?' He threw his hands in the air. 'You're considering sleeping with him. *Perfect.*'

'Abhijeet! One word and I will slap you.'

'What one word? Go say that to him. Why? What happened? You can say anything to me, but not to him. He is the one who's making you cry. He is the one who treats you like shit. He goes out with other girls and you don't say a thing to him. He doesn't love you, I do. He doesn't . . .'

'Enough. I am leaving,' she said, as she gathered her bag, wiped her tears off and turned to leave.

'Yes, go, go to him, sleep with that rich fancy bastard with the big car. I don't care about you. Go away, go sleep with the whole college, I don't care! I don't know how you came here. Did some rich guy pay for a management seat here? I hope you fail your exams and I know you will, anyway!'

'What?' She turned back. 'Abhijeet, just because you have some big placement doesn't mean we all are worthless. And what are you? You were nothing when I met you! You were nothing but a bookworm and a nerd! I made you what you are . . . *I* did or otherwise you would have been still roaming around the college alone, eating Maggi with your head buried in your books.'

'At least I am not a gold-digger and a slut!'

'What?' At this, she hit him with her handbag repeatedly, while breaking into tears and howling at the same time.

Abhijeet stood there, realizing what he had just done and slumped on the pavement with tears in his eyes, as Riya walked away from him.

Crushes on friends are always disastrous, and so was this one.

After that incident, Abhijeet just wanted to get through the remaining few days left in college as quickly as possible. He tried to date a few girls in between, but it never worked out. He was surprised to see how comfortable he had got around the opposite sex.

Days were long and laborious as he waited for a time when he, too, would be rich, and would dictate terms in a relationship.

Silverman Finance meant new opportunities for Abhijeet. But for Shruti, it meant a new life, away from her previous one. It pains me to think of the life Shruti led before Silverman happened to her. So, before my eyes well up and bring out the tissues, let us go to that moment in time when she had another sad day in another sad month in another sad year of her sad life.

2

She wiped the sweat from her brow. Jagjit's face flashed before her eyes as she entered the room. Her hair was neatly tied in a ponytail behind her neck and she had chosen a crisp white shirt and slim trousers for that day. With her naturally pouted lips, gorgeous legs, the five-inch stilletoes, the razor-sharp features, the high jawline, and a stomach so flat that it would put a road-roller to shame, Shruti could easily have been mistaken for an exotic Indian model on a rampway.

She was nothing like her parents, both fat and ugly-looking. Except maybe her complexion and she would thank them for it. The thought of dark chocolate, sweet-smelling skin still makes my hair stand on end. Shruti used to be one of the most sought-after girls in college; her body-hugging cotton fitted shirts and the knee-length skirts were the talking point for many discussions in and around college. Nobody could fathom how she fell for Sachin, the college's stationery shopkeeper's son.

'Good morning, Shruti.'

'Good morning,' her voice cracked.

'You want to drink something before we start?' She nodded, picked up the glass and emptied it. 'Why finance, Shruti?'

'I have always been interested in this field, sir. I have done CFA level one and CA foundation level. I have also done my internship at Morgan Stanley and Barclays. It is in the file. Everything is in the file. The college certificates, too. I also won the business quiz at DCE. I won the Business Plan contest and the singing competition and the math quiz and the entrepreneurship seminar,' she said and opened the file and thrust the certificates out in front of him. She was panicking.

'I don't need to see those. Why Silverman Finance?'

'Sir, it is because it is the best financial institution in the world and I really want to work there,' she said this and her mind drew a blank. She just sat there, rubbing her hands and looking down at them. The fear of failure choked her.

'And?'

'Sir, that is the reason. I really want to work at Silverman.'

'Or is it the money?'

She stared blankly at him. Her head spun like she was in a revolving chair.

'Yes,' she said.

'Just the money?'

'No, sir.'

'Then?'

'Yes, sir. Sorry, sir. But I am ready to work hard,' she said, her voice failing her and her head starting to spin again. 'Sir, I have scored well here and I will do well there, too. I promise. Just give me a chance and I assure you, I will do well. Sir, I promise. I worked hard all my life and will continue doing so. You can check my results and my performance in academics are as good as my extracurricular activities,' she was almost begging.

'Calm down, Shruti.'

She nodded furiously as she felt it slipping through her fingers.

The kind interviewer gave her a few minutes to relax, and then asked her questions about balance sheets, accounting principles and taxes, and she breezed through them. The interviewer made sure that her exemplary performance in school and college were not a sustained fluke, and that she was truly the brilliant kid her marks suggested. Studies, exams, college rankings were the only things that she cared for in her god-forsaken life. She had made sure that *that* part of her life was perfect.

She walked all the way home that day. The walk back to her place meant a lot to her. It had changed her life. Had her father not seen Sachin put his hand across her on the way back home one day, she wouldn't be getting married this year. The walk didn't really decide what would happen to her, but it brought her fate closer than it had been previously.

'What took you so long?' her mother asked, as soon as she stepped into her house.

'The interview went on for very long,' she said, as she made her way to her room.

'It is eight. Do you think we are fools? Where were you?' she asked as she grabbed hold of her hand.

'I was in college.'

'Then why didn't you pick up your phone?'

'I was in the interview.'

'All the time?' she asked. 'I will not tell your father this time, but the next time you are late, I will tell him, and then *you* face him.'

'Whatever,' Shruti shrugged off the threat, stormed into her room and threw her bag on the bed. Her mother followed her into her room. Shruti did not have a room of her own till she was eighteen and had to share one with her brother. After a month of discussion, the storeroom was cleaned up and she was shifted there, despite earnest requests from her brother that he wanted to take that damp, dark, squalid minuscule room. Her brother had his tenth boards that year. Shruti was slapped for persuading her brother to ask for the storeroom.

'Next time you talk to me like that, I will throw you out of this house. Then go into Sachin's arms and do whatever you want to. Ever since you have met him you have forgotten all about us. That lowly bastard!'

'Mom.'

'Shut up, Shruti. And keep your tone down. You are such a selfish daughter. You have no responsibility towards the house. Look at your room. Don't you have eyes? Have you ever bothered to clean it? We don't have twenty servants here to do the job. I have to do it. You don't realize how much you take us for granted. No matter how much freedom we give you, you still want more. And what do you give us? Your grandmother has been coughing for the last three days. Have you bothered to ask her how she's feeling? All you want is your college, your job, your career, your friends. This is the last time I am telling you, Shruti, forget about the job and don't you dare say a word about that in front of your father or Guptaji. It is your luck that you are getting such a big man to marry you.'

'He is a divorcee.'

She got slapped. Yet again. Her mother's shrieks filled up the room.

'So what? That girl was a witch. She didn't know how to cook. Even took up a job. What do you expect? A wife of such a rich man to work? They have done a lot for your father and for whatever we have done for you, you have to keep him happy. It will be shameful if you do anything inappropriate there. But what do you care? All you think about is yourself. Even if we die, I don't think you will shed a single tear. Why don't you kill us yourself instead of putting us through all this?'

Moms are quite brilliant at this. I do not know where they get it from, but they have this innate capability of pulling out everything from the closet. You spill milk today and you will be shouted at for not scoring well in a maths exam that you took five years ago, thereby spoiling the family name.

'But I have done nothing to get him. I don't deserve him.'

'Shruti!' her mother shouted and slapped her again. She started howling and crying. 'How dare you answer back to me! They can take away this house. It is mortgaged to them. You know we are neck-deep in debt, don't you? How can you be so insensitive? My own daughter? How can you? I wish you had died at birth. At least I wouldn't have to see this day.'

She kept sobbing, a little softly now. It always worked. Shruti felt a tinge of guilt in her heart.

'I will do what you say,' she mumbled.

'No, do whatever you want. Kill us. That is what you want, so do it. I am ashamed to have a daughter like you. Don't talk to me. Go and make rotis now,' she said and left the room as the bell rang. It was Shruti's father.

Shruti started making rotis and overheard the conversation between her parents, which was deliberately loud so that she could overhear what they were saying.

'I am sure she will blacken our faces some day. And that is after everything we have done for her. I always knew one day she would turn her back on us,' her father bellowed. 'I am sure she was with that bastard. She is so brainless to not think of Jagjit as an opportunity. He likes her so much and she is such a waste. Call her.'

Her mother called out to her loudly.

'Yes,' she said tremblingly. She wished her brother was around. She wouldn't get hit then. She stood in front of her father, who looked drunk and in a foul mood.

'Shruti, this is going too far,' her father said. 'Just because we have given you freedom doesn't mean you will exploit it. I don't want to know why you were so late today but I have decided something and you will have to do it. No college from tomorrow. You will go to Jagjit's place and talk to his mother. It has been three months since we promised to get the two of you married and they have not seen your face up till now. What impression do you think you are leaving on them? I do not want to hear any excuse. You have studied enough. Nothing will come out of it. Anyway, once you get married, you are going to sit at home and serve him.'

'But Papa . . . the marriage is a year away.'

'Don't you dare answer back. You will do what I ask you to do. You get that? Go to your room.'

'But I want to do this job till the time I get married.'

'We are not discussing it,' her father said, as he sipped his whisky. He was a big, fat, balding old man, who, in his youth, had stood tall as a light pole and strong as a boulder. His word was the rule. People feared him. But then, times change. A few business deals went awry, he lost his reputation and people lost confidence in him. That was when Jagjit's father lent him money for a business that failed, spiralling him into debts worth crores, and he drowned himself in alcohol. For now, the only place he was still feared was in his daughter's heart. His hand was heavy and she knew that.

'Why not? I want to do the job. It's a once-in-a-lifetime opportunity.'

'Why? You are not going to do it all your life. Help your mother till the time you get married. Help her out. She is getting old and you still suck her blood. Look at her. Don't you feel pity, growing fat and roaming around with boys while she works in the kitchen all day?'

'I thought it would help in the dowry.'

Her father looked at her in sheer disbelief. 'What? A two-paisa job and you will pay for your dowry? Don't act smart with me,' he said mockingly.

'It is thirty lakhs per annum.'

'What?' her parents echoed. Her father gulped down the whisky, and his pride.

'Show me the offer letter,' her mother said.

'We will get it tomorrow,' she said.

'Then we will talk about it tomorrow.'

She walked to her room, closed the door behind her and pinned her ears to the door and listened to what her parents had to say.

Their tongues had started wagging. They were now hatching plans of how they would not tell the Gupta family that she was working, and instead would tell them that she was at her maternal grandmother's place, taking care of her. She closed her eyes and wished she could run away.

Hyderabad.

She prayed.

The next day, with her hands lathered with detergent, she picked up the phone. It was from the placement cell. They told her that she could come to the college and collect her offer letter for the job at Silverman Finance. She wanted to jump and dance and run around and tell everybody; instead, she cried. It took a while for the news to sink in and when it did, she smiled as widely as she could.

Everything seemed to change around her. Her eyes, always sunken, now had a twinkle in them. Her walk had a spring in it. The only thing that did not change was her brother's love for her.

'Run away,' he said.

'What are you saying?'

'Run away,' he said again, as he closed his book. It was his board exams that year. Cable connections had been cut. Computer wires had been taken apart. Shruti's protests that these steps were not taken when she took her board exams were looked down upon with scorn. She was slapped and told how selfish she was.

'I am serious, Didi. They will get you married here and you know that.'

'Yes. But there is nothing I can do,' she said as her mind raced with possibilities.

'Yes, you can. I am sure they will let you go to Hyderabad. They want the money and you know that. You don't have to take it any more. Once you settle there and have a few months behind you, stop sending them money and refuse to come back. That is it,' he said. It was a brave thing for him to say at his age.

'It is not possible. You wouldn't understand.'

'I understand everything, Didi. Dad will run into trouble with Guptaji, with loans to pay. But what has that got to do with *you*? You can't push yourself into this because our alcoholic father and overspending mother led themselves into a horrible life. Didi, the day I get into an engineering college, I will forget I ever had parents.'

'What are you saying, Archit? They love you.'

'They do? I don't think so. And even if they do, it is because I am their son. They know that I will sustain them once I get a job. After that, they will marry me off and torture the girl to death for money. I am not going to be a part of all that.'

It was almost as if the two of them had switched ages.

'Don't say that. They have brought us up and . . .'

'So what, Didi? Every parent does that, and they have done nothing special. You were pushed inside the kitchen when you were six and Mother spent all her time watching television. Dad could spend on his whisky while I had to wait months for a new bag. I got it eventually, but had it been you, you wouldn't have seen it ever. Just because they fed us for all these years doesn't give them any right to govern us. I am tired of all this.'

'But what if I lose the job some day? Where will I go then?'

'You will not, Didi. You know you are good. And even if you do, you will find another one. And in any case, I will start earning in a few years. There is nothing that can go wrong here.' He smiled at this.

'What? Why are you smiling?'

'Didi, you are beautiful. Even if you don't find a job, you will find someone worthy enough of you, someone rich, very rich. Grab him, and he will shower you with everything you might need. Things will be just fine. I can't wait to see you with a big diamond on your ring finger,' he said and started laughing.

'Shut up,' she said, even as she was crying.

'Why? You still love Sachin?' he asked.

Sachin was the son of the stationery shop owner at her college. He used to photocopy the books Shruti couldn't afford to buy, and slowly, they came close and fell in love. After her father saw them and Sachin saw the bruise marks on Shruti's face the next day, he stopped coming to the shop, and Shruti never saw him again.

'I don't,' she said, as she wiped away her tears. Some relationships are strange. Sachin and Shruti hardly ever talked or met, but they knew they could spend a lifetime looking at each other and smiling shyly.

Just then, their parents entered the room and the conversation stalled.

Ever since her dad had brutalized Shruti after spotting him with Sachin and Sachin had vowed that he would never see her again, Shruti made no efforts to trace Sachin and neither had he.

~

Three months passed since the call from the placement cell, and that day she found herself standing at the airport, her parents struggling to find words to bid her goodbye. While she was issued warnings about staying away from boys and what would happen if she didn't, she was also hugged and they said that they really cared for her. Her parents knew this was a gamble, sending her to a different city, with no supervision and lots of money. But they had taken months to decide that they would let her go. They had made their calculations and it fit right with their plans. It was worth the risk. And the money.

She disappeared behind the clearance gates, looking back once at her brother, who smiled and winked at her.

Run, her mind said. And she ran.

So, while Shruti had been counting the days right up to the day she would finally leave *that place,* and time hardly seemed to pass, for Saurav, time was running out ... quick.

Still a virgin, his school friends studying engineering abroad were doing it as frequently as he changed clothes and he wasn't feeling any good about it. Although I think he was a lucky son of a bitch, he didn't think so.

One of the few things that you lose, or you don't, when you are in IIT: your virginity.

3

How many times has it happened that you looked at a rich kid getting down from a big car and wished you were him or her? What would you do if you *were* him or her?

One thing you would NOT do is—study. Study till you feel your eyes would pop out.

But what if no matter what Saurav did, be it staring down at his teacher's cleavage as she bent or staring up his classmate's skirt, he used to retain everything that was taught in class, and no matter how hard he tried, he ended up doing very well in his exams. Even by IIT, Delhi standards, he was insanely intelligent.

To cut it short, Saurav was unwittingly brainy and enviably rich. Saurav had been born with a silver spoon in his mouth. He was the new generation—educated rich. Life was an extended dream for him.

It was unfair to the world when he got through Silverman Finance without even breaking into a sweat. But he wasn't too concerned about his career, for he had bigger issues at hand to take care of.

Freud once said, *if you don't lose your virginity before twenty-four, you will always be a loser*. Or someone said something like that. His friends from school had warned him about it when

25

he cleared the entrance examination for IIT, but he didn't pay heed.

Samrat. Kapoor. Kiran. All his guy friends were neck-deep in women within the first few months that they landed in Holland, the US and the UK respectively. He was still a virgin.

They took out time to send him pictures of themselves in parties with beer glasses in hand and half-naked women in their arms. While all he did was send them scanned copies of his nine-point something IIT mark-sheets. They all had almost the same future ahead of them. Just that while they fucked, he got fucked!

'I am just waiting for the right time. I can't sleep with just anybody,' Saurav said unconvincingly.

'You are a *guy*! We can sleep with anybody with long hair and breasts. Just go find a girl!'

'But it would be the first time. I want it to be special. I can't just ...'

'Don't give me that crap, man. Every time that dick of yours goes into something wet, you will feel special, trust me! Just go ahead and stop fooling yourself with the virginity bullshit. It is not the 1800s.'

'It is not so easy here. And I am not the smartest around here and you know that.'

'I do, man, but there must be one girl, at least one in the whole of Delhi who can think about sleeping with you, dude! You just have to find her; she won't come to you. And you are a rich guy, man! You drive your own Audi, you're an IITian and stuff! Girls love all that, trust me.'

'But where do I find these girls, man. All my friends are even bigger nerds than I am. It's not that I can ask them to set me up.'

'Anywhere! Join cooking classes if you have to and lay an aunty. I don't fucking care, but do something about this.'

'I will try.'

They hung up. His inferiority complex touched new heights every time he talked to his friends.

Saurav was five-ten and looked shorter. He was girlishly fair and weighed a staggering 120 kilos and looked more. It had been years since he had seen his toes. He wasn't cute and plump; he was fat.

As soon as he got through Silverman Finance, he joined a slew of classes to find a girl who would look through those layers of fat and see his pure, love-craving heart within. Maybe even his dick. Or at least get clicked pecking him. Or hugging him. Anything!

Guitar classes. No success. There were too many guys smarter, sexier and thinner. Dance classes. He was too fat to make an impression, and he realized his body wasn't meant for freestyle jazz.

Finally, he was among his own breed when he joined the gym. Fat, flabby bodies sweating on treadmills and crosstrainers, struggling with small weights on bench presses and Smith machines, men and women alike.

He looked at her. She was on a treadmill stacking up miles and was too big and flabby to be missed. Some would call her cute because of her fat round face, which was as fair as it could realistically get, and slit eyes.

'Hi,' Saurav said and tried hard not to pant while walking on the lowest speed on the treadmill. The girl looked at him, smiled and kept walking. After a while, she stepped down from the treadmill, walked up to the nearest couch and flopped on it.

Saurav followed her.

'Hi.'

'Do I know you?' The girl asked, wiping her face with a towel.

'Umm . . . no. But we can know each other.'

'Excuse me?'

'I mean, I have been noticing you for a few days and I think you are incredibly cute.'

'That is because I am too fat to look smart or sexy.'

'I beg to differ,' he countered.

'Isn't this your first day here?'

'So, you have been noticing me, huh?' he asked, trying to sound sexy. It certainly didn't work. A fat man can't talk like James Bond and get away with it. I say it from experience.

'Obviously. You are the fattest around here. I felt good when you walked in. It's good to see people who are fatter than you.'

'Okay,' he said, disappointed.

'Don't worry. A few months and you will be as thin as me!' she laughed. Saurav found that cute.

'I hope so.' More than actually laying her, he was imagining how their wedding photographs might look like.

'Hmm . . .' She took out a water bottle and took a sip.

'Can we go out some time? Like coffee or anything? If you don't mind?' he asked, his fingers crossed.

'I do mind. But then, I have nothing else to do after this. So how about now?'

'Perfect,' Saurav said nervously. He couldn't guess where this was going but he decided to play along.

They both changed into their regular clothes and moved out of the gym. While Saurav had hidden everything under the triple XL tracksuit that he was wearing, Megha was bursting out of her jeans and T-shirt. Saurav, nonetheless, found her attractive and immensely desirable.

At twenty-two, it was his first date. Not that Saurav was shy, but the very fact that it seemed like he was pregnant with triplets killed his chances with any girl. And IIT hardly gave him time to lose that weight or be around girls.

'What do you do?' she asked him.

'I am studying. IIT Delhi. BTech,' he said.

'What? You're an IITian? Are you kidding me?' she exclaimed.

'No, I am not,' he said and fished out his ID. It was his explanation to all his goofiness and awkwardness: his IIT Identification Card.

'I don't need that. But seriously? IIT? You don't look like that. I mean I don't want to offend you, but you look like a property dealer's son or something.'

'Why do you say that?'

'You know. You're fat, you drive this huge car and everything, and flirting with me. An IITian doesn't necessarily do that.'

'When did I flirt with you?'

'You did.'

'I didn't,' he protested and thought maybe he did.

'Whatever.'

'So, where are we going?' Saurav asked. He was really counting on his chances now.

'You tell me. You asked me out.'

Samrat's words echoed in his ears. Samrat used to tell him how easy it was to have a first date at home, have a couple of beers, and then casually make out.

'My place,' he said in a very low tone, hoping the honk of the car would drown it out. *I was kidding*, he would say if she were to make a face at that, he had decided. And then he would laugh and she would laugh and they would go to a coffee place.

'Cool. Let's go,' she said in a heartbeat.

Saurav blanked out for a few seconds and it took time for it to sink in. *It's just an innocent date at my place, don't panic*, he told himself. He started thinking about what reasons there could be for a girl to come to his place. Was he cute? Was she lusty? Did it even mean anything? Was he thinking too much? Was the gymming already working?

He parked the car in the driveway and walked past the wide-eyed guard who was shocked to see Saurav bring home a girl. They went up to his room and he cleared his bed of the laptop and his books that were strewn about and asked her to sit. He was tongue-tied and words refused to come out of his mouth; he was sweating and he was nervous as hell.

'Do you want to drink something? Eat something? Should I get you a beer?' he asked. She nodded. 'Pizza?' he asked and she nodded.

He rushed downstairs, pulled out two large beers from his father's stash, called the pizza place and asked for a large, extra cheese pizza. His heart was throbbing out of his mouth as he entered his room again and gave the bottle to her.

'Nice,' she said and she chugged on the beer. 'It's a little strong though.'

'Yes, I know,' he said.

The girl started to talk about how she hated going to the gym and how much she loved eating and Saurav nodded like a child. She asked him about his days at IIT and whether it was as tough as people made it out to be. Saurav, still dizzy and nervous, answered in short sentences. After a while, the bell rang and Saurav fetched the pizza.

'I don't think I can eat that,' she said. 'I am already very full.'

'Are you sure?' he asked, as he stuffed a slice into his mouth, cheese dripping from the corners of his lips.

'Can you switch off the light? It's piercing my eyes, Saurav,' she asked him. His head started throbbing, and with trembling hands and a pounding heart, he switched off the lights, his mind racing and conjecturing as to what would happen next.

They both sat on opposite corners of the bed. Saurav finished his beer and asked her if she needed more. She shook her head.

'So?' the girl asked.

'Umm . . . so?'

'Why did you want me to be here?' she asked and looked at him. He felt embarrassed and shy and naked. I don't know for sure what happened next, for I have never been told in explicit detail, but I think they kicked off their shoes, stripped, and probably broke the bed. They made out like animals, leaving behind aching love bites and worn-out muscles. Saurav had done bloody well for his first time. After they were done, they finished the pizza and ordered another one.

The picture he clicked had her kissing him on the cheek while a bedsheet covered their fat naked bodies up to their necks. They kissed and exchanged their byes, after which he looked at the picture and cursed himself for clicking just one. He dropped her home that day and the smile never went off his face.

Later that night, he shot a mail to his friends with that picture as an attachment. He waited for their replies.

Bravo! But isn't she a little fat?
Cool! Now we are all men in our group.
Made for you, man! Are you going out with her?

He smiled and looked at the photograph again. Was he missing her? Already?

~

The next day, he waited in the car at a distance to catch her before she entered the gym. He couldn't stop thinking about the previous evening and he wanted to relive that experience. He put the car in gear as soon as he saw her getting down from the auto and walking towards the gate of the gym.

He screeched the car right in front of her and waved at her.

'What? Are you crazy?'

'Yes, about you,' he shouted. 'Want to go out again?'

'Not today,' she said and disappeared inside the gym.

He parked the car and entered the gym to find her on the same treadmill. She looked at him entering the gym and continued running. He, too, ignored her and walked to the leg press machine instead. The leg presses felt a little heavy on Saurav legs, as he saw her smiling at the guy running next to her. The wait for the treadmills around her to be vacated was getting longer as the conversation between the guy, who was probably the trainer, and Megha was punctuated with laughter and smiles.

Saurav shrugged it off his mind. He chose another treadmill and started running as fast he could. However, the noise and the vibration from the rickety treadmill didn't make her look at him as he had hoped.

After a few bench presses and ball exercises, the trainer left her, for he had to train a girl who had come in shorts and a bursting sports bra.

'Hi,' Saurav said as he sat down next to Megha.

'Hi.'

'So, what are you doing today?'

'Nothing.'

'So, can we go out and have coffee or something?'

'Or do you want to take me to your place again, huh?'

'Ummm ... It is your call. Whatever you want to do.'

'Your place,' she said. Saurav was a little shocked because just a little while ago she had behaved like she didn't know him. They went back home and this time they didn't order beers or pizzas and there was no awkwardness; they made out again and he dropped her home.

He emailed his friends about his second time and they called the girl names. Bitch. Slut. Whore. It made him angry.

'Oh! You are my man! You have got yourself one horny bitch, man. So cool! Finally, I am so fucking happy for you, man. Very nice!'

'At least don't abuse her, man. She is a nice girl.'

'Ooo, I am sorry but she *is* one horny girl. She came to your place two times in two days! I am so proud of you. Make sure you use a condom dude, you never know whom she is sleeping with!'

He didn't pursue the conversation any further and decided that the next day would be a date that didn't require her to come to his place, a date that didn't end up on his bed.

Why? I have never understood Saurav. Make hay while the sun shines. Even when it doesn't. Just go out and make hay. Which perfectly normal guy would prefer a date over a make-out session?

The trainer and Megha were laughing their guts out when Saurav reached the gym the next day. He wasn't in his tracksuit; instead, he had picked out a pair of jeans he thought he looked thin in, and he had fixed his hair with copious amounts of hair gel. He had dressed up for a date.

Saurav made his move after the trainer went off to help other members.

'What are you doing after this?'

'Nothing? Why? You want to take me to your place again, you pervert?' she asked and giggled.

'No, actually I was thinking maybe we could go out for an early dinner or something?'

'Hmm, okay. I will just go and change. But it's on you, right?' she laughed.

She took a shower, changed into her clothes, and hugged her trainer before she left the gym with him. Saurav wasn't too happy to see that. It was envy, not love. Saurav was a fat man, the guy was a hunk, probably better in bed. Saurav stood no chance.

Saurav took her to the most expensive restaurant he had heard of, and I am sure he was thinking of going somewhere the trainer would not have been able to afford. It was a nice dimly lit restaurant, probably very classy, and insanely expensive.

'So, what else?' Saurav asked. 'What do you do the whole day?'

'Nothing. I am doing correspondence from Delhi University. So I am at home all the time.' She sipped her lime juice.

'Pretty boring, huh?'

'Yes, but can't help it. That is how I am getting so fat. I just want to get over with my graduation and do an MBA from some place. At least I will get to see a college. It gets so frustrating sitting at home the whole day.'

'Get a boyfriend. That is a nice timepass.' He said that just to check whether she had one and if not, what she thought about having one.

'I already have one,' she looked at him and smiled.

'*You have one?*' Saurav asked, shocked.

'Why do you look so shocked? He is in the US. That is why it is so boring. Had he been here, it would not have been that bad.'

He struggled with words as the word *slut* rang in his head. 'What does he do there?'

'Nothing. Doing some course on business or something. He went there to have fun and nothing else. I am sure he is never going to pass it. Whatever.'

'How many years has it been that the two of you are in a relationship?'

'It will be three next year.'

'So, what are your plans with him?'

'Nothing. He will come back next year, and then within two years, we will get married or something. You tell me? Any girlfriends? Or is that prohibited in IIT?' she laughed.

'Yes, I have one. She is not in the city . . . Umm . . . she is in Bombay,' he lied.

'So, how much time has it been for you?'

'Just a few months. I don't believe in serious relationships.' He didn't know why he said that.

'Me, too.'

'Three years and you say you don't believe in serious relationships? You're one heck of a non-believer, aren't you?'

'I don't. It is just that after a year into any relationship, it is the same. There is a sameness.' To this day, Megha remains my best character in the story because she understood relationships. She continued, 'It is just that you fight less in a long-term relationship and that is the only parameter of a successful relationship. You get used to that person around you and you don't want to hurt him or her. That is why relationships work. It is like somebody cuts off your cable subscription or internet connections. You throw a fit. But really, after a while, everything becomes okay. So yeah, when the person you love moves out, there are withdrawal symptoms, but you survive it. Isn't it obvious? You start loving a person more than your best girlfriend in a matter of days and you are ready to leave her for him. It is just that being in love is an idea which is so beautiful. Plus, your girlfriend doesn't have a dick. Your best buddy doesn't have breasts. He won't tell you how good you are. My friend won't tell me how beautiful I look. We need someone from the opposite sex to do it, to satisfy our ego, our needs. That is what love is: a desperate need to feel good. Love is an illusion, nothing more, nothing less.'

Ever since I heard this from Saurav, I have used this speech more than a few times on brokenhearted girlfriends and distraught boyfriends. The guys start looking for someone better. The girls don't understand. That's the universal rule.

'So you don't love him?'

'I don't know. It just feels nice sometimes that he is there. Plus, instead of marrying someone you don't know, I would rather marry him. He is an okay person, doesn't drink or smoke. He will join his father's business and has a secure future. He loves me, too, I guess. So, I don't think it is too bad a deal.'

'*Deal?*'

'Yes, why not? Arranged marriages are deals, aren't they?

You choose the best possible match. A compromise between looks, family background and economic strength is struck and then you marry him or her. This isn't any different. He is the best I could have got with all the flab hanging around. I am set for life.'

Saurav had nothing to say. I had nothing to say when Saurav narrated this to me. Had he described her to me as someone even remotely attractive, I would have fallen in love.

'Okay.'

'I am sorry for that. I just said what I wanted to say.'

'I think you made sense,' he said. Saurav, at this point, had started comparing himself to her guy.

'Shall we leave? Mom would be expecting me.'

'Sure.'

Saurav dropped her home and told her that he had had a good time. She repeated the same.

He went home that day and deleted the picture from his cell phone and computer.

Calling her a slut a million times in his head didn't help, as he thought he was falling harder for her with every passing second. He was damn lucky he came across her or he would have still been a virgin.

Saurav missed the gym the next day, as his internship had started.

He called her from his office but she did not pick up. The gym trainer's image kept cropping up in his head while he sleepwalked through all the sessions organized for him that day. He kept calling and messaging her throughout the day, but she did not revert even once.

~

The next day, he missed office and went to see her at the gym. She seemed to be having a good time with the trainer, laughing and blabbing with him. Saurav's temper rose, but he still walked up casually to the closest couch and sat down there.

After the trainer got up and attended to the thinner, hotter girls, Saurav came up to her.

'Hi.'

'Hi,' she said as she grabbed her things and walked past him. He followed.

'You have not been picking up my calls.'

'I know,' she said as they walked out of the gym.

'Why not? Did I offend you in anyway?'

'I was busy,' she said casually, not looking at him.

'You could have sent one message.'

'I didn't get time,' she said coldly.

'For *one* message?'

'No, I mean I was really busy. Don't irritate me.'

'Where were you busy?' he asked, as they both paced towards an auto.

'My boyfriend was in town, I had a late night the day before and was very tired the next day.'

'And yesterday? You were tired the whole day?'

'I went out with Amit,' she said as she haggled with the auto-driver.

'Amit?'

'The trainer.'

'You went out with him? Why? *Why?* I mean, you see how he flirts with all the girls in the gym. He is not a nice person. How can you even talk to him?'

'Look, Saurav. Don't tell me what to do.' She got inside the auto. 'And let me decide who is nice and who is not. I am doing whatever I want to. I am not answerable to you.'

'You just slept with me. Yes, you are answerable to me and I love you.'

'No, you don't.'

'Yes, I do,' he said frantically.

'Buzz off.'

'You want a deal, right? I am richer than your guy. I am an IITian for heaven's sake and my parents are motherfucking rich. I will be with you,' he shouted.

'Are you drunk?'

'No, I love you.'

'No, you don't. You think you do because we made out. But you don't.'

The auto had went off leaving behind a cloud of dust and haze. Saurav told me he felt really stupid after that.

~

He stopped going to the gym, deleted her number, and deleted all pictures of her. He had no choice after she had stopped picking up his calls and had changed her gym timings and instructed the gym people to refuse to tell him when she came.

Time flew by and he forgot about her. There were withdrawal symptoms but he managed to cope with them, just like Megha had said.

The twist came after two months when she called Saurav and told him that she had broken up with her boyfriend of three years. She asked if they could meet up and Saurav turned it down, though the prospect of making out again with her was almost too tempting.

Whatever happened, it did Saurav a world of good, though. He had finally *done it* before twenty-four, before he was a college graduate. Hail Freud!

He got close to getting into a relationship a couple of times after that. He almost kissed one girl.

The first girlfriend, the first love, the first boyfriend and the first fling. Take these seriously for there is always something to learn. I learnt how not to get dumped. It is amazing how many different ways you can get dumped, and I know of six from experience.

Anyway, Saurav at least learnt something. *Don't* go out on *proper* dates when you can have it three times on three days. You never know when times change. However, he still thought about her but that was only when he had to fantasize. He had moved on.

4

Garima was sitting in her room when the results were announced. She looked out of the window wordlessly and thought, maybe it was the way out of her wretched luck.

Hyderabad.

She went back to scratching her chipped black nailpaint off her fingers. It had been three years since her nails had seen any other colour. No, she wasn't a heavy metal fan. She wasn't a punk or a gothic girl either, though her sheer disdain towards dressing up and an affinity towards the colour black suggested otherwise. For the last three years, she had worn unflattering, loose T-shirts with dirty jeans and chappals. Her frizzy brown hair was always left open and her eyes always had kohl smeared carelessly by her roommate, Aditi. Aditi also used to do all of Garima's shopping, overloading her wardrobe with all the girly stuff that she never wore, getting her accessories that she never put on. But Garima never stopped Aditi from doing so. At least Aditi felt good about it.

Aditi had tried more than a million times to draw Garima out of her quietness, but in the last three years, nothing yielded. Garima was herself only when she was drunk and she had made a habit of it.

Apart from that, she was fine with the emptiness around her, and no matter how hard people tried to get close to her, it never worked. She was a nice person otherwise, helping anyone who needed to be helped, but that didn't mean she would be friends with them.

There were a lot of things that worked for her: her smile, which she flashed only if someone did anything stupid; her face, beyond the kohl, fair as the moon and glowing; her dark brown hair that she never thought about cutting. Guys often fell for her, but her cruel disinterest used to break their hearts into a million pieces.

She wasn't always like this. She used to be a normal girl.

Everybody has break-ups. So what if she had had one?

That is what everyone used to say.

Garima, about three years ago and days after her board results came out, had caught Karan kissing some other girl, right in front of her eyes, and her world had instantly crumbled. She could have got into any college in Delhi, but she chose Chennai. Away from her home, friends, the few she had, her family and Karan.

Her family resisted, but they couldn't stop her from going. She was never refused anything by her family. She was born after her mother's earlier pregnancy ended in a stillborn twin brother and sister. When she came into the family, their business saw money like it had never seen before and she was always thought of as the reason behind it. She was loved beyond measure by everyone in her family and her word was the first priority. Despite all this, she was hardly spoilt, her demands were rarely extravagant, and her demeanour always sweet and amenable.

In fact, she rarely asked for anything and took the bus to school like everyone else, while her personal Honda CRV, along with a driver, did not see the light of day. Karan took the same bus every day and they sat together, till the time Karan thought it would be better if they went to school in her car. It would give them more time together, he said.

Garima never thought it was right to hide things from her mother, so she told her everything about Karan and her mother didn't say a thing. Right from the day when Karan asked her out on Valentine's Day to the day he first held her hand, everything was known to her. The subsequent developments were quite obviously never discussed, though her mother politely asked her to be careful and to go slow.

Her mother never liked Karan, but neither did she have the heart to tell Garima so. Garima was the happiest when Karan proposed to her and her mother was happy to see her daughter smiling and hopping about. The next day, Garima gifted Karan a gleaming new cell phone. Her mother said nothing.

They were so much in love, or maybe only she was. Karan never reciprocated as much as Garima did, but then he couldn't possibly match up, Garima thought, as she loved him so much. Karan came from an upper-middle-class family while she was filthy rich. Garima had her own credit card before she was fifteen.

Everybody knew about the two of them as the ideal couple. Garima was fair and had fuzzy, long hair which reached a few inches below her neck. She stood tall. She had inherited her height from her mother and the hours spent at the basketball court had toned her body to a bikini-perfect state. She had toned legs, a flawless fair complexion and a rock-solid body, and she was one of the fuller girls who were just the right weight.

And by what I know about Karan, he was pretty good-looking too. But whatever.

They were envied, praised and loved.

They were both extremely brainy and often fought for the top position in class. The time that Karan spent at her home often rivalled the time he spent in his own. Her parents were slightly miffed at her when Karan and she spent hours sitting in her room with the door shut, when they were supposedly studying, but they kept silent because they had nothing against Karan. Nobody had anything against Karan. He was a feet-touching, high-scoring, good-looking kid whom everybody loved, from teachers, to friends' parents to grandparents.

Though he never did anything out of the ordinary, he never

pulled back his words on how much he loved her, and how much he wanted to be with her. He was very smart in these matters.

Anyway, no matter what everyone thought, Garima did every ridiculous thing in the book to keep him happy. One casual mention about the PlayStation his friend Ketan had got himself and the next month anniversary, he got that in his hands. No matter how fervently he tried to keep her from giving him these gifts, Garima relentlessly made sure he kept them.

As months passed, Garima's life started revolving around Karan. She, who once had friends all over, all the time, had just one name governing everything in her life. The friends were slowly left behind; the groups she was in continued without her and she didn't have any problem with it. She spent her days sitting at home and thinking about him. Garima stopped seeing any point in going out with her friends when she could go out with him instead. All she thought about was him. She woke up with his name on her lips and slept with his name in her heart. Her heart still skipped a beat when she saw his name flashing on the phone. Garima slept every night clutching the cell phone in her hand, just in case he called. Her pulse peaked whenever he said he loved her. The world seemed a much nicer place when he was around.

She never wanted anything from him. She was just glad that Karan was around to take care of her. Karan worked on extremes. He ignored her right to the point where she would be moments away from tears. And when that happened, he would come up with great lines and some flowers to make her fall in love with him harder.

Prerna, her best friend once, and now only friend, often warned her against her obsession with Karan, though it hardly mattered. Best girlfriends have always been the biggest enemies of dirty boyfriends.

'Garima, I think you are going too far,' she said on her now very infrequent visits to her place. Garima had stopped going out unless it was with Karan. Though, he preferred staying at home . . . for obvious reasons.

'Why, Prerna?' Girls often lose all sense of reason in love.

'*Why?* Which girlfriend gives her boyfriend such an expensive watch? It is ridiculous.'

'But he wanted it, Prerna. He wanted it so much.'

'Guys want everything. You can't go on giving him anything and everything. Tomorrow he will drool after a BMW and are you willing to buy him that, too?'

'I will buy him whatever I want to. And yes, if I have that kind of money, I will buy him everything that he wants. It is my money, why do you care?'

'You are so rude,' Prerna said, as she gathered her books to leave.

'So are you.'

'See, Garima, I have nothing against you. All I want to tell you is to be careful with Karan. He has been showing off things that *you* bought him, as *his* own. And this I know for sure. That iPod you gifted? He denied that you had given it to him. I swear on my mom. But you do whatever you feel like. Just that he was also spotted with Ritika, the one from the science section, a couple of times. Just open your eyes for heaven's sake.'

'Whatever,' Garima said and stared at her book, her eyes already turning away from even the thought of it.

'Whatever.'

Prerna left.

Garima started crying. She was livid at whatever Prerna had just said and she was already imagining him with Ritika.

I don't know Karan, but why would anyone, I mean *anyone*, leave a hot, rich, girlfriend who lets you into her bedroom, to go out with some average-looking girl? We are a strange species. Us, men.

Going back to that day, Garima sat there crying, weighing whether or not to ask him about Ritika. After an hour of deliberation, she called up Karan. He kept rejecting her calls as he said he would. The next day was Garima's birthday and the board result celebration and he had said he would be busy preparing for it.

She called up his friends and the third one gave away the venue of the surprise party. The place was a five-minute drive from her place and Garima drove over in her night suit, only to regret doing so.

She caught Karan in the parking lot with Ritika.

Kissing.

~

No matter what Karan did afterwards, it made no difference to her. She was leaving for Chennai. Three years away from her home, that house, that city, that bedroom, that car, and the world she lived in.

Away from everything.

It was only after the break-up, that she realized she loved him more than she had ever imagined. She cried for days, stopped eating and harboured suicidal tendencies. She felt used and cheated. Her world had crashed right in front of her eyes. She thought it would take a lifetime to build it again. She was wrong.

Love is not what you live for. Love is what makes it a little easier.

5

M onday, 4 August.
8.00 a.m.

I will not bathe.

Snooze.
8.10 a.m.

I will not shave.

Snooze.
8.20 a.m.

I will take a cab.

Snooze.
8.30 a.m.

What the fuck?

Turns off alarm.
9.30 a.m.

Great. Up before the alarm. Not bad for the first day, Saurav told himself and reached out for his cell phone, a swanky new N96, a phone he had seen the Roadies, the bickering contestants of a popular reality television show, carry. He wondered why his phone said six missed calls. Then he saw the small clock on the top of the screen.

9:40.

9:40?

What the fuck? How is this possible?

The alarm didn't ring; he was sure.

He got up in a flash, cursing the phone for its meek, powerless bullshit speakers.

'Does it have FM and an alarm?' That's what his mom asked him when he had bought this brick-sized phone and told her about the GPS navigation system. If only he had taken her seriously. He shaved. He took a bath. He couldn't afford to look bad; he wanted all the attention he could get from the girls. He had seen gorgeous banker girls in the movies and he couldn't possibly miss out on them!

He put on his new white and blue striped Louis Vuitton shirt and slipped into his pinstriped Hugo Boss trousers, and a tie from Ermenegildo Zegna.

Saurav had lost a lot of weight since the days of Megha, but you still wouldn't call him thin, fit or anywhere near that.

He patted his paunch and cursed IIT, for it had made him fat, which it had. He checked his tie for the last time, and ordered a cab. He kept his hands away from the sandwich which was left over from yesterday. Today, for the millionth time he thought, he would start dieting.

He was ready for his first day at office.

And was late by forty-five minutes. Already.

10.15 a.m.

The cab would still take fifteen minutes.

Last week had been a wild goose chase across the length and breadth of the city to find a suitable house. So much so, that it had almost spoilt the whole fun of staying at Taj Banjara, the last word in luxury hotels, which was paid in full by Silverman

Finance. Three gyms, two pools, breakfast buffets, super-hot hotel management grads, et al. He had asked a few of the housekeeping staff for their numbers, but it didn't work out. Even saying that he was an IIT graduate didn't help. *Sluts*, he told himself. To get back at them, he stuffed all the shampoos, soaps and combs into his bag before he left the hotel.

Anyway, he had managed a flat, at walking distance from that hotel, quite ironically.

Saurav had already started missing Delhi and the beautiful Delhi girls. They were more receptive to *I-am-from-IIT-Delhi*.

'*Naye ho, sahab?*'

'*Haan.*'

'Twenty minutes to reach there,' he said with a typical Hyderabadi accent.

'Just be a little quick,' he said, as he opened the newspaper. It was a great feeling. Only if the car would have been a Lexus and his own. He had refused the car his dad offered to take to Hyderabad, saying that he was good enough to buy one of his own!

He put the newspaper aside and started fiddling with his phone. A good thirty minutes later, they reached a maze of huge buildings and wide roads. If Delhi traffic was bad, this was worse. Nobody shouted or charged at each other with iron rods, but they were pretty much banging into each other all the time!

10.45 a.m.

He was an hour and a half late. It was 11 a.m. when he saw the building from a distance. The building was as humungous as it was beautiful. Steel and curved glass formed an imposing structure and its monstrosity made him feel terribly insignificant. I remember going through the same emotion. A big building. A taller woman. They all do that to you; they intimidate you.

As Saurav's car approached the entrance, the top of the building was no longer visible. There were a few honks from cars nearby and a smug-faced guard appeared and said something foul in a south Indian language. Saurav, too, abused, just to retort.

'Sahab, you have to get down outside only. Only personal cars allowed,' the cabby said. Saurav got down and paid the cab-driver who drove away. Seven hundred fifty bucks for a cab ride and he would still be seen walking to the office! He still wasn't out of his awe of the building when he saw something else which left a lasting impression on his mind.

The driveway.

The car right behind him was an Audi.

The car right behind the Audi was a BMW 7 series.

The car next to it was a Mercedes C class.

And the car which he almost banged into, a Honda CRV.

He would buy the Audi, he made up his mind. He was not a big fan of Asian cars.

~

An hour earlier, Abhijeet was standing where Saurav was now.

Abhijeet had stood outside the door for a few seconds, taken a deep breath and let it out. It was a new *him* entering through those doors, those doors that led him to a new life, which had fame, success and money at every step.

Saurav swung open the revolving door and strode in with a big smile, looked at everybody who walked past and smiled at them. I remember *seeing* him then. He looked funny and fat, even in his expensive clothes.

After a few seconds of awkwardly looking at the huge empty space in front of him, with his mouth half open, he started looking for the reception. The ceiling of Silverman Finance is about fifty feet high and the place is brightly lit in a brownish yellow glow accentuated by the same coloured marble below. It is an insanely huge hall. One walk around the Silverman office and you start feeling small. It's practically an entire city inside an office.

He walked up to the far corner of the huge hall, where the reception was. Saurav peered across the huge wooden desk, shining as if it had been polished just a moment ago, behind which were seven people manning it, headsets on their ears and a big smile over their faces. All of them beautiful, their lips shining with gloss.

A large sign hung overhead, with bright yellow lights shining behind it.

Silverman Financial

'Excuse me. I am Saurav and . . .'

'Good morning, Saurav. Here is your access card. Go straight and take a left. Swipe your card, this way up. Take the lift to the second floor. Go straight and take the third right. You will reach the training room.'

He thought of asking for her number but she had gone back to staring at her computer screen and smiling at it. He crossed the waiting area which was more like a movie theatre, only that the seats were much better and the LCD screens were a shade smaller. He stood there, eyes fixed on the screen watching CNBC, just because the ambience was so riveting.

Just as he was about to lose all sense of time, he was knocked right in by the hurried *click-clocking* of high-heeled women and Cuban-heeled men all around him. It was a sea of expensive fabric, banned leather and exotic perfumes. People glided across the floor in Hugo Bosses, Armanis and Versaces with Louis Vuitton either hanging from their shoulders or making their feet look beautiful.

Of whatever Saurav knew about brands, he picked up the most expensive of clothes that Delhi had to offer. Yet, on him, they were made to look like tatters. Everyone was tall, insanely well built, immaculately dressed and most of them looked American or European with a tan gone wrong.

Women had their hair tied tightly behind their heads, making their skin seem like taut membranes stretched over their cheekbones. This smoothed out their wrinkles. As for the men, their suits shone, their shoes glistened and their watches glimmered. Their heads shone. Some of them were half bald. The rest had theirs slicked with gel in trendy hairstyles. They had sacks full of money to spare and it looked like they spent it well.

He cursed the men, and wished the women were naked. He smiled at them and they looked at him with disgusted expressions on their faces. He swiped his card, rotated the stiles and entered the lift lobby. Twelve lifts, six on each side, a few of them opened, a few closed. The whole floor was sparkling clean. Brown marble, golden plated lifts glistened in the neon lighting and huge mirrors covered the walls.

He chose the lift with the fewest people in it. The lift was a room in itself, including a two-seater sofa. *For what? For making out?*

While he waited restlessly for the lift to reach the third floor, people around him were busy digging into their BlackBerries and PDAs.

The lift doors opened and he breathed easy.

He left the lift lobby and saw the same figures he had seen on the ground floor. They were sitting amongst a sea of the same kind of people, with their eyes glued to their computer screens. Nothing moved, no one talked. Yoga sessions are louder. Saurav remembered the instructions. He walked straight towards the training room. What he was wearing on his wrist or on himself was no longer exclusive or above par. Everything was pedestrian, his phone was an embarrassment now. His shoes, a joke. His slight paunch, a calamity.

He rushed across the floor, taking small but fast strides, eyes on his feet, trying to avoid attracting attention. A penguin among humans. He felt more eyes turning towards him, sighing and turning away.

Saurav finally felt relieved when he saw in bold letters: *Training Room*

6

The second day of training had started on a very peaceful note, unlike the first, when a stern-looking female who stood three inches taller than Saurav, asked him to go back home, as being late was something which was not tolerated at Silverman Finance. He had to leave the room and the office building, and it was not quite the start he was looking for. That day, he was the only person sitting in the room, fifteen minutes early.

A few minutes later, a few badly dressed men and women—boys and girls, more precisely—walked in, fidgeting with their hair and watches. Within the next fifteen minutes, the room was filled with twenty people selected from twenty elite colleges. All of them were overachievers.

The conversation between them shifted swiftly from how much they had scored in their graduation to the bigger things they had achieved in their lives. The St. Stephen's College girl had forgone a master's at LSE to join Silverman Finance. The IIT Mumbai graduate was an IIM (A) dropout. One IITian had a patent to his name, something called a brain oximeter, and wanted to look for investors in the company. The girl from Delhi College of Engineering was a national badminton champion, apart from being a gold medallist in various Olympiads, both national and international. The girl from Presidency was super cute.

An easy silence hung in the room. Everybody was trying to keep conversation to the minimum and I wouldn't be telling you this story had Abhijeet not picked the seat next to Saurav that day.

The whispers died down and everybody sat up in their chairs as a click-clocking sound approached the door. Saurav wanted to ask Abhijeet if the same female who had come the previous day would come in today, too, but pulled back, seeing him freeze.

She walked in, the woman who was to haunt them for the time to come.

Sumita Bhasin. Chief HR. Silverman Finance.

Her perfume invaded their nostrils and violated their sense of smell. What Saurav hadn't seen the day before, he could see then. Sumita was colossal, almost twice the size in every dimension of an average Indian woman. Or man. She leaned over the table they were sitting on and ran her eyes through the room.

'Seems like everybody is present today,' she said, smiled and showed her big teeth jutting out from blackened gums.

Saurav momentarily made eye contact with her and found her repulsive.

Sumita was approaching fifty and was fighting hard to keep it away. She had the familiar hairstyle that let her hide her wrinkles. Her wrinkles were not done in by the monthly Botox shots she took, which bloated her foot-long face and made it look even more sinister. She hardly smiled; the last plastic surgery which stretched her skin from nose downwards had left little scope to do that. She stood taller and was wider than most men around her, especially with four-inch pencil heels, which, over the years, had made her veins jut out from her feet and made them look even uglier.

Sumita had been working in the firm since its inception and swore by the company rules. She was very uptight and tolerated no slip-ups and made life hell for whoever flouted the rules. She wielded almost absolute power and had to just go one level up to get anybody she wanted out of the company. Her voice was raspy, her words, harsh. There was not one girl who hadn't been reduced to tears by her cutting words. The men had it no better.

She called for an office boy who got twenty hundred-page manuals for them.

Campus to Corporate, it said in bold letters.

'I want you to go through it before we proceed,' she said. Her voice, like a man's baritone, grated. It sounded like she had a perennial cold. But that took nothing away from it, in terms of volume. When she whispered, the whole office could hear what she had to say.

They started flipping through the pages. Most of them started underlining what they thought was important. Geeks!

But no one dared to smile.

It was a detailed account of how they were expected to behave at SF, how they were expected to dress up, how they were to address people and the like. It even had addresses of places they could buy their clothes from. Silverman had a design consultant for clothes right in their office.

Saurav started nudging Abhijeet to show him something he found amusing and Abhijeet asked him to shut up a little more loudly than he would have liked to.

'You think it is funny?' Bhasin asked scornfully, pointing at them.

'Who? Me?' Abhijeet said, already sweating all over.

'Yes,' she said, hands on her waist, head leaning forward, her eyebrows making a hill on her forehead and anger writ large on her face.

'I was reading it, ma'am.'

'First lesson you learn at Silverman Finance,' she leaned back and looked at all of us. 'We are smarter than you. And every joke played here is on you. Not us.' She reverted her stare back to Abhijeet and asked, 'What did you find funny, Mr Abhijeet Gupta?'

'Nothing, ma'am.'

'What did you find difficult enough not to be understood on your own?' she asked, and her voice rose with every sentence.

'Nothing, ma'am.'

'Out of the room.'

'Ma'am?'

'Did you not hear me, Mr Gupta? You think we are all fools here to have made this manual? Look at yourself. Does anybody here think he looks like the people working outside? They are all professionals there and you have to be like them. And it is my job to get you there. There or out of here.' She banged the manual on the table.

'But—'

'It was me, I was asking—' Saurav butted in.

'OUT!' She pointed towards the door. 'Leave the building. Right now. And that is for both of you.'

'Okay,' Saurav said and promptly collected his stuff to leave. Abhijeet had no choice but to follow him out of the room.

'If you still behave like college kids, this is how we are going to treat you. The only difference is, you lose a job here and not some grades. It's up to you.' She stared at them, waiting for the fear to register. 'To start with, let me tell you very honestly,' she said and got up from her chair. 'Each one of you today, here, is a disgrace to our company.' She smiled to show all of her upper jaw, and rubbed her hands together. Her long red painted nails shone. 'Every one of you may have topped your college, but that accounts for nothing. We are all toppers here and that's our minimum criteria. *You* would not be here if you were not academically brilliant. Anyway, now that you are here, there are just a few simple rules that you need to follow. They are given in this manual.'

'I assume that nobody gets these things now,' she said and continued, 'However, there is one advice that you could make good use of. Every slip costs us. We don't tolerate that. We are giving you money that nobody else does. We expect that back. And more. That is business. The day you slip, it would be good for you to update your CVs and look for new jobs. We do not tolerate incompetence. Only the best stay. The best are very few. Thank you and have a great day ahead. And if Mr Abhijeet or Mr Saurav talks to anyone of you, tell them they have already taken a step in the wrong direction. Out of this place.'

She picked up her handbag and left. The group stared at each other, red-faced as they thought about what she had just said.

Soon after, the training lectures started.

It was 10 a.m. then. They sat in the same damned position for the next sixteen hours, except for an hour each for lunch and dinner. It was getting tough even for people who were used to studying sixteen hours a day. These were people who were academically the most brilliant in the country, these were the most tireless and intelligent brains of the country and they were tired out by Silverman in a single day.

By the time that day got over, it was 2 a.m. and their bodies were stiff and most of them wished that day was an exception, not the norm. They had heard about demanding schedules of investment banks, but they had no idea the rigour would start so soon.

Silverman wasn't going to pay them for doing a nine-to-five, cushy job. They wanted the last cell of their bodies to work for them till it died and decayed. The only good thing left about the job was the pay cheque, now that they knew they would be working their asses off for it.

Apparently not.

~

After they were thrown out, while Abhijeet was embarrassed and felt like sitting and brooding over it, Saurav was already in the lift lobby. He waved at Abhijeet like a mad man. Abhijeet walked up to him, head bowed as he thought about what had just happened. It wouldn't do much good to his days there, he thought.

'I am really sorry for that. That bitch,' Saurav said as they both entered the lift.

'It's fine. Not entirely your fault.'

'Saurav.' He put his hand out.

'Abhijeet.' They shook hands.

'Where do you live?'

'Madapur.'

'Okay.' A few more minutes of silence passed between them. 'Is there a problem?' Saurav asked him.

'No,' Abhijeet said, still not looking.

'I am sorry for what happened in there.'

'So am I,' Abhijeet responded.

'I tried to take you out. It didn't work out. I said I am sorry, but you still look pissed off.'

'So what do you want?'

'Nothing.' Saurav was a little taken back at the rudeness of the whole conversation.

'Great.'

'Do you drink?' Saurav asked, almost mocking.

'Occasionally,' Abhijeet replied, looking up for the first time in the whole conversation.

'Let's go.'

'It's on you,' Abhijeet said, and for the first time Abhijeet smiled, albeit very slightly. They took a cab home to Saurav's place, which wasn't that far away now that the early morning office traffic had cleared up.

'Your flat is HUGE!' Abhijeet exclaimed as he spent five minutes gawking at just the living room. Abhijeet's place opened with a washroom on the left and a kitchen on the right, and had two tiny rooms and three people shared it.

Saurav had an ice box with two crates of beer in it, with every single beer in place.

'Nice place,' he said again, as Saurav showed him around his flat.

'Thank you,' Saurav beamed and they clinked their bottles and poured the beer down their throats. They started talking about their colleges, their friends, and found they had more than a few things in common. For one, Saurav couldn't believe that Abhijeet was a shy, nerdy guy in college.

'You have no idea how big a geek I was,' Saurav said.

'You? A geek? But you're rich! Look at this flat, Saurav. If I were as rich as you, I wouldn't pick up a single book in my life,' Abhijeet conceded.

They both finished their bottles and then another one and they were tispy because both of them weren't regular drinkers.

'Do you drink often? This crate and the ice box?' Abhijeet asked, with bloodshot eyes.

'Looks good to have an ice box and everything. Very occasional. Plus, the first girl I kissed was drunk when it happened, so it's like a fail-safe, a lucky charm. So you tell me, why did you get so worked up today?'

'Nothing. It was just . . .'

'Yes?'

'It is just that I really want to make it big here. This is my chance to get rich and maybe have a house like this, you know. This job means everything to me,' Abhijeet said with exaggerated hand movements.

'C'mon Abhijeet, if not this then something else. There are a million jobs out there, man.' Saurav took another swig at the bottle.

'I am not an IITian like you. Nobody is dying to take us in. Jobs are few and far between. And ones like these? Once in a lifetime. I lose this, twenty years of slogging goes down the drain. I will be just like any other graduate.'

Saurav smiled inside on hearing the IIT part and said, 'What crap? You are good, you are intelligent. You would get through a good company in no time.'

'My dad, college topper. What does he do? He works for the government for peanuts. Why? He didn't take chances or lost them. I am not going to do that. I will make this work, come what may. I will have three cars in my driveway before thirty, have rings on all my fingers and have three servants serving me while my wife blows all my money up in a beauty parlour. When people look at me, I want them to crave for a life like mine. I want them to wish they were as rich as me.'

'Whoa! Whoa! I think you're drunk already!' Saurav said and they both laughed. 'I think I am too and this is the first time I am drinking in the morning.'

'Me too,' Abhi answered.

'So you're here for the money. People would call you greedy and materialistic,' Saurav argued.

'People who already have three cars would call me greedy.'

'I have three cars,' Saurav answered.

'You do? Do you think I am greedy?'

'Actually, I have four cars and I don't know whether I would call you greedy because I don't know what it's like to be you,' Saurav said. 'Oh. Wait. I should write that down, that's borderline philosophical.'

'Thanks, Saurav. But remember, some day I, too, will have four in my driveway.'

'I am sure you will,' Saurav said and they both lay down side by side on the floor.

'And I will have three girlfriends when I have money,' he said. 'You know why? Because all girls love money. When I will be rich, they will all be flocking to date me!'

'I have money and no one is lining up to date me,' Saurav sighed. 'Maybe we are just losers and we are meant to die alone and rich.'

Both of them drifted off to sleep.

The next day was a holiday. It was Guru Purnima but both of them kept hanging around at Saurav's flat since they had not activated their official mail IDs because Sumita Bhasin had thrown them out of the office and they missed the orientation lectures given by the IT Department.

The next day, they were called by Sumita to her cubicle and were given an earful for missing office the day before, without informing anyone. Apparently, the cab waited fifteen minutes for them. They were called irresponsible, unprofessional and everything that could be said in the limits of office decency and were reminded that their days might just be limited in Silverman. The first three days had gone horribly wrong for Saurav, but he was more sorry for Abhi and apologized profusely.

The training classes only got more exhausting after the first few days. Going to office became a drag and the entire batch lived their lives from one Sunday to another. Their life was reduced to an unchanging back-breaking schedule. Get up at seven, reach office by eight, attend lectures till two in the morning, come back home and sleep. They had absolutely no time left for anything else. The two weekends that went past were consumed by sleep and exhaustion. Their frustrations crept up with each passing second, but they had no choice; this was the life they had chosen for themselves. It was two weeks to their first salary and that was the only thing they looked forward to. At least they were being paid amply for all the inhuman torture they were going through. It would all be worth it after they got the pay cheque, they'd thought.

Two and half lakhs. Both Saurav and Abhijeet had plans; Saurav had eyes on a Tissot watch. Abhijeet wanted to gift his parents a foreign holiday. Still, they would have enough to last six months.

Life was about to get better.

Or maybe not.

7

It was the last day of their second week in Silverman. Just as they got up to leave, a sweet-looking man from the HR department came and addressed everybody in a very sweet tone, rubbing his hands together and smiling ear to ear.

'Good evening, everybody. I am Tarun, from the HR department. I hope you have had a good time up till now. And that we have come up to your expectations.'

Nobody answered and a few rolled their eyes.

'It seems like all of you are very tired, so I will come straight to what I need to tell you. As you know, Silverman has very high standards and strict quality guidelines, and it is expected that you reach that level. Since you are all fresh out of college, you have a lot to learn and imbibe in terms of knowledge as well as how the corporate environment works. It has been decided by the management, purely because all of you are very raw and inexperienced, and not because you are not worthy enough, to put you all in an advanced internship programme.'

Everybody woke up and listened closely.

'It is nothing to worry about. It's just a standard procedure. The internship programme is nothing but an evaluation of where you stand and how you have worked in the last six months.' People started looking at each other and tried to find someone who was not surprised and knew what this was all about. Everybody sat up, all eyes set on him, hearts in their mouths.

He continued, 'After six months, every one of you will be evaluated and only then will you be a permanent employee in this firm. A few of you will have to say goodbye to the firm . . . that is, only if you don't perform.'

Their pulses shot through the roof. They were being pitted against each other. Their hearts sank and they started to sweat. They were being evaluated.

'Bullshit,' Saurav said out loud.

'Quiet, class. If you have any questions, Ms Sumita Bhasin will clear them out. But first, somebody will come and give you the letter that stipulates all the conditions of the internship. Go through it, sign it, and submit a copy to me. My cubicle number is 783. And yes, till the time you don't clear the programme, the remuneration given to you will be just your basic salary. That is because you would be under the training module and not essentially adding anything to the company. Thank you for your time. Everything is in that letter. Do go through it.' He left and closed the door behind him. It was followed by pin-drop silence in the class.

The circular was distributed and the mood was sombre. Some of the girls were in tears. The revised salary was seven lakhs. Their basic salary, down from the thirty they had been offered. No watches. No foreign holidays. Everybody sat with head hung low, as they thought about what lay in front of them. Seven lakhs, of the thirty promised.

It wasn't worth it any more. Twenty-odd years of hard work had withered these people away. Each one of them had spent days brooding behind closed doors, cursing themselves for every mistake they made whenever they came second in class. These people had beaten themselves down for every exam they didn't top, every medal they missed.

All they had accumulated all these years were some papers with numbers on them, a few medals, a few certificates. This was the time all that hard work would have meant something. They felt robbed.

They deserved what they had been promised.

They were crushed. The last six months, they had daydreamed about this day, when the many years of hard work would pay off and it would all be even. They'd missed movies, they'd missed friendships, they'd missed relationships, they'd missed parties, and ultimately, they'd deprived themselves of all the fun for this one day. The day they would race ahead of the lot. The day it would all be even. However, it did not happen. Their dreams were shattered, their hopes crushed. Silverman had not just taken away their promised salary, but had also stamped under its corporate foot, twenty years of their young lives.

Shoulders drooped. Some of them cried, some leaned back into their chairs, slouched and ran over the last six months in which they had done nothing but think about this day. Abhijeet sat there open-mouthed. He felt cheated. Humiliated. Saurav kept swearing. Abhijeet didn't even have the heart to tell his mom about this.

The only consolation that the circular provided was that a month later, a few of them were to be taken to Singapore for a training schedule. That gladdened them, but the word 'few' reminded them of the choppy waters that lay ahead. The person next to them could cost them a training trip to Singapore and possibly the job. Before people could start knowing each other, a big wall was drawn up between them. Everyone was competition now and the field was set.

'Wonder how much I would be earning had I not been greedy,' Abhijeet looked at the ceiling and sighed. He would have been working at HLL, like the guy who came second in class.

'This sucks, man,' Saurav said as he looked around to see faces hung in disappointment.

Everyone wanted the money. That is what jobs are for. Money. Of all the new joinees, it was Shruti who went through the letter most frantically, time and time again, hoping the letter would change.

'Unfair,' Garima said and rocked in her chair.

'Huh?' Shruti said, her mind still blank.

'It is very unfair, I said.'

'Yes,' Shruti said, her eyes wet.

'We could have done better. A lot better. Are you okay?' Garima asked her.

The class started leaving. Garima waited for Shruti to say something, but Shruti just stared at the letter as her eyes got wetter. She didn't even blink. The whole class had left but Shruti kept sitting there. Like a corpse. 'Yes,' Shruti said.

'You want me to bring you something. Water?' Garima handed over a bottle to her. Shruti broke down, dug her head inside her palms and wept bitterly. Garima put her hand on her head and tapped it soothingly. Half an hour passed by the time she stopped crying.

'Thank you,' Shruti said.

'For?'

'I don't know.' Shruti walked, still dazed. She stumbled over chairs.

'Are you sure you are okay? You don't look fine to me. You want to sit in the cafeteria?'

'I don't want to stay in the office.'

'Come to my place,' Garima said.

'My parents won't allow that.'

'They don't have to know,' Garima argued. Shruti broke down again and Garima insisted that she spend the night at her place.

They took a cab to Garima's place and Garima gave her pyjamas to wear. Garima asked her to choose a top for herself from the wardrobe. Shruti was still crying in small bouts, cursing her luck, and cursing Silverman Finance.

'I haven't really unpacked, but you can choose anything to wear from my closet,' Garima said.

Shruti peeked into the wardrobe and for the first time that evening, her expression changed. It brought a twinkle to her eye. She stood there, rummaging through the tonnes of fabric Garima had stashed in her cupboard.

'Do you like anything?' Garima asked apologetically.

'I like *everything*. I have never worn anything so . . . nice . . . and expensive . . . You really have nice taste and lots and lots of clothes.'

'Actually, my friend in college bought all my clothes for me. I have never worn most of them.'

Garima noticed that everything Shruti wore was stitched. No labels. But she still managed to look smashing. The pyjama she gave Shruti seemed like it was made for her. Not that Garima was fat, she was miles away from it, but she lacked the supermodel legs that Shruti had. And she lacked the brown-chocolate-fantasy complexion.

'You can have anything you want,' Garima said. She felt a sudden surge of liking towards Shruti. She spent the next hour dressing Shruti up in the finest of her tops and dresses and felt good about it. Shruti obviously had no qualms about getting into clothes she had never dreamt of. If two girls can share their clothes, they can share almost everything.

Beyond everything, the only thing I could think about when they narrated this incident to me was whether Shruti changed in front of Garima or not.

Tired, both of them lay down on the bed, laughing and giggling.

'You can keep anything you want to,' Garima said. 'I am serious. I don't wear any of this! And I am anyway too fat for any of this.'

'Oh, c'mon, Garima, you're not fat. You're so fit! I'm too skinny. And I can't just take it like that. They are yours,' Shruti said, even though she wanted to say yes.

'You can. I don't wear them anyway. I will be happy if you take them,' she said, as she lit up a cigarette.

'Why do you smoke?'

'I like to smoke. I can't sleep if I don't smoke, I can't wake up if I don't smoke, and I can't even function if I don't smoke. I am basically handicapped without my cigarettes. Also, if you're smoking, you can avoid conversations with people.'

'I should stop talking then,' Shruti said.

She stubbed the cigarette out. 'Aw! You can talk, I allow you to.'

'Conversation is a two-way street. You have to talk, too, just in case.'

'Start,' Garima said and smiled at her.

Shruti spent the night telling her about everything she had gone through. Garima cried more than once as she told Shruti about Karan and told her how she always thought life had been unfair to her. Garima told her not to worry about anything and that things would be alright. They both felt sorry for each other and hugged each other to sleep.

Garima woke up the next day to a hot cup of coffee, French toast and freshly cut fruit. For Shruti, domestic chores was a way of life. They went out shopping that day, Shruti wanted to dust Garima's place but Garima insisted they go out.

'That is looking great . . . that blue really suits you,' Garima said.

'It does? Why don't you buy it, too? We will both have it then. Won't that be cool?' Shruti gushed.

'I don't like dressing up,' Garima conceded.

'Why not? You would look much better than you look in those loose jeans and the dull oversized T-shirt,' Shruti argued.

'There is no one to dress up for. Try this . . .' Garima handed her a yellow summer dress.

'Then find someone!' Shruti shouted from the dressing room and laughed. 'How is this?'

'Great. We will take both and I am paying,' Garima said.

'Garima . . . I don't want you to pay.'

'Zip it. Just this time, Shruti. You can pay me back by setting me up with a cute boy. Once you do that, we will find you a rich guy!'

'Yes, right,' Shruti said sarcastically.

'Why not? Any guy would love to have you. So we will find you a rich guy, just like your brother said.'

'I would rather turn, you know, lesbian and let you pay for me.' They giggled.

'You will find a guy, Shruti. Nice and rich and someone who

will love you. It is the best career option, you see. Better than Silverman Finance. We can then go shopping every day and we don't have to care about Ms Bhasin or internships or Jagjit Singhs.'

'Why don't you find yourself a nice, cute guy? I am sure you would have plenty of them around you.'

'I just can't trust anyone now,' Garima sighed.

'Aw! Don't worry, we will find you a poor guy who will find it very tough to live without you. But I think I will settle for a rich one.' They both laughed.

'Done! Rich guy for you,' Garima said.

'Nice guy for you,' Shruti said and they laughed again.

Garima ended up buying the first of the girly, frilly stuff for herself in years, and she admitted that she liked what she had bought.

8

As if Silverman Finance wasn't enough, they were making it tougher for themselves. It had been a week and a half since the announcement and everyone tried harder.

Classes were longer now. They all wanted to stick around. Everybody concentrated. Everybody asked questions. Everybody was back in their college frame of mind and they were giving it their all. Notes were taken and filed and coffee was gulped in ridiculous amounts and water was splashed on faces at every break.

They were exhausted. Many of them skipped breakfast and a morning bath just to get a few extra minutes of sleep. Tea breaks were replaced by short naps. A few of them puked and felt dizzy, but it didn't matter for it was a race and they couldn't afford to lose.

'Do you want coffee?' Saurav asked Abhijeet, who was going through his notes.

'No. You go ahead. I have to read this thing. I just can't wrap my head around these debt structures. This whole thing is so complex.'

'C'mon, Abhijeet. You can take a break. Five minutes won't make a difference.'

'It might. I don't want to get into more trouble and you're like the black hole; you invite trouble wherever you go.'

'Whatever.' Saurav looked away.

'Okay. I will come, but only five minutes and then you will make me understand this.'

'Five minutes only and I will teach whatever the fuck you want me to teach you,' Saurav said. 'By the way, first salary today. Want to go out and celebrate? It's been so many days and we haven't even seen what Hyderabad is like!'

'We will talk about it later.'

They were back just before the lecture started. Everyone sat with the bottom of their spines touching the back of the chair. Nobody dared to blink or look at their watches or cell phones as the Wharton-educated, Ermenegildo Zegna suited man talked something about enterprise value and comparative analysis in his heavy American accent. He took breaks to tell them how he rose in the company to become its Managing Director.

Managing Director!

He was hardly forty and looked younger than most of the people working outside.

'I know it gets tough here. However, you will get used to it. Let me tell you, this is the honeymoon period. You can either make money or lose it. Right now, you are expected to do neither. So you can enjoy yourselves. I know it's a stupid thing to say to you when you work eighteen hours a day, but this is the reality of investment banking!' he said and smiled, quite sympathetically.

It had been eight months since Thapar had shifted from the US office to India to head the department and people had mixed feelings about him.

'The more we work, the more credit he gets.'

Thapar gave the US office everything they wanted and expected from the India office. People were working late hours, weekends, Sundays and national holidays, and they were getting paid for it. The employees were free to leave the company any time they wanted to. It was fair.

Thapar was a sweet talker. It was hard to dislike him and even harder to argue with him. He was a godfather for young people, a friend for people of same age and people older than him were either in awe or in envy. He was there to stay. I never liked him, though. I don't like men who are better than me and especially if they have the hots for a girl named Avantika. You will know who she is in due course of time.

He continued the lecture and now questions poured aplenty. Every time a question was asked, Saurav gave Abhijeet a disgusted look. Abhijeet ignored Saurav and would be busy writing everything down.

The girls were trying desperately to get his attention. By now, they had noticed that Thapar was undeniably charming. Peppered hair, chiselled features, a pointed nose and a tanned European complexion, not to mention, immaculately dressed. He looked like an Indian Daniel Ocean from the *Ocean*'s trilogy.

Thapar left and left everyone behind, discussing him.

~

'What did she say?' Garima asked the two guys who were known to get into trouble with Sumita Bhasin.

'Excuse me?' Abhijeet said.

Abhijeet and Saurav were again called up by Sumita for some disciplinary issue.

'I could have killed her,' Saurav butted in, banging his fist on his palm.

'Was it that bad? What is her problem with the two of you? Someone told me you were called to her office before as well? Is that true?' Garima asked and Abhijeet nodded.

'She is a bitch,' Saurav cursed.

'Shut up. He is here,' Garima said as she opened her notebook.

The trainer for the day was from the IT department and was there to make the joinees familiar with the various information security issues.

'Do you think he heard us?' Garima asked.

Abhijeet had not been able to take his eyes off her from the moment she came and sat next to them, even though he was embarrassed that she knew that Saurav and he were already labelled as the troublemakers of the group. Abhijeet had always noticed her sitting in the opposite corner of the class.

'I don't think he cares. Probably he agrees with what we think of Sumita,' Abhijeet said.

The class started and the IT guy started stressing on the importance of passwords and other related topics. *All mails are tracked*, they were told, inviting scorn from many.

They were relieved when he said the class would end early. Nobody showed it but every one of them envied the jobs they had once looked down upon. They envied their friends who were back home by seven every day, while they slogged till two. Though, nobody said it. They had heard stories of how speaking against the firm often resulted in unpleasant things. Sumita took special care of them and no one wanted to get on the wrong side of her.

The class went on and everyone kept fighting to keep their eyes from closing shut and headaches.

Movie today? Ask her too. If you can. Saurav wrote on his pad and passed it on to Abhijeet. Garima peeked in and noticed what Saurav had written. There was an awkward silence before Abhijeet scribbled on his notebook and shoved it in front of Garima.

Abhijeet: *Movie today? Salary celebration?*
Garima: *You will not get the tickets. BTW, which movie?*
Saurav: *Any.* Wolverine? New York? *And why won't we get tickets?*
Garima: *3 halls in Hyd. All seats are booked in advance. Don't even try.*
Saurav: *Dinner?*
Abhijeet: *Where?*
Garima: *Little Italy. Have heard about it. Free beer thrown in.*
Saurav: *I will ask other people. U ask the girls.*
Abhijeet: *Hehehe.*
Saurav: *I was asking Garima.*
Abhijeet: *Ohhh!*
Garima: *Wot? I don't even know them.*
Saurav: *You don't even know us.*

Garima: *Whatever. I will ask the girl from SRCC. She is sweet.*
Saurav: *And the girl from Presidency. Please?*
Abhijeet: *Hehehe.*
Garima: *Wot do I get?*
Saurav: *Chocolate.*
Garima: *Dark. And no nuts.*
Abhijeet: *Hehehe.*
Saurav: *Shut up.*
Garima: *Shut up.*
Abhijeet: *Why? You need 2 concentrate on Information Security?*
Garima: *Bad joke.*
Saurav: *Terrible.*
Abhijeet: *Presidency? Bad choice.*
Garima: *Terrible.*
Saurav: *Abhijeet—blind, Garima—jealous.*
Abhijeet: *Shut up.*
Garima: *Shut up. I don't even know you.*
Abhijeet: *Hehehe.*

~

'What will you guys have?' Shruti asked, as she had no clue as to what to order. Garima had asked Shruti and she was only too glad to join in. She had never stepped out alone in Delhi after sundown and she was really excited.

'Not much of a drinker, are you?' Saurav said as he poured over the menu card.

'Not at all. This is my first time,' Shruti said. Although they were all depressed because the salary credited to their accounts wasn't even half of what they deserved, but they had decided they wouldn't talk about it.

'Never mind, Shruti, even we don't drink. I have started very recently and anything that I drink gets me tipsy,' Abhijeet said.

'And you?' Garima asked Saurav.

'I have been drinking for quite some time now. But I never go overboard. Just beer and that, too, very occasionally. Anyway, let us do it today. Let's go overboard and get really really REALLY drunk. It will be fun.'

They called the waiter.

'A pitcher of beer. Abhijeet?' Saurav looked at Abhijeet for his approval.

'I don't think we will be able to finish it,' Abhijeet said.

'Make it two. I will help you guys,' Garima said.

'Oh, you drink?'

'Why don't we just wait and watch,' she smirked.

The waiter came and Shruti bombed him with questions, much to the embarrassment of Abhijeet and Saurav, while Garima just laughed throatily.

'How bad does it taste?'
'You will mix it?'
'Lime cordial? What is that?'
'Will it make us puke?'
'Don't get us too much.'

The waiter could barely keep from laughing.

Salsa chips, garlic bread platters with extra cheese, chicken fresco and pastas were ordered. Shruti and Garima promptly cut out the cheese and mayonnaise parts and Saurav called them losers.

A little later, their table was overcrowded with bottles, glasses and plates full of food.

All of them had been geeks all their lives. They had been the only ones who, even after the last exam of the year, would go back to their rooms and match with a textbook whether their answers were correct. After every result, they checked the margin by which they had beaten the person who came second.

And that day, they lay sloshed outside an insanely expensive restaurant in uptown Hyderabad. The alcohol had hit all of them except Garima, who drank the most, even mixed drinks, but was still comparatively sober.

'You know what?' Saurav looked at others and said, 'I am going to run this place some day. I am telling you, dude. I will run this place. This sensex . . . this sensex, it's going up all because of me. And that bitch, Sumita, I will kill her. No seriously, I will kill her. Abhijeet will help me do that. My best friend. Don't think I am drunk. I am not. *Tu jaanta hai mujhe nahi chadti.*'

'*Haan, bhai. Abe saale*, if you run this company, what will I do? Let me run this company. You have four cars in your driveway, anyway. And only nice girls like the two of you will be allowed in our company. Will you work for me, you two beautiful ladies? May I have the pleasure of having you work under me?' He bent his head down till he fell over.

'Abhijeet. Abhijeet. Listen to me. Abhijeet. When are you asking Garima out? Tell me? She needs a nice guy like you!' Shruti asked out of the blue.

'Shut up,' Garima said, smoking her fifth cigarette that night. She sat there, not saying a word, smiling at people who were looking at the drunk trio.

'Why? Why should I? I am not nice. I am not even rich. First, I will get rich. Then I might just think about it.'

'But please do. She will be waiting. She likes nice guys. She told me. We have a deal. If I get her a nice guy, she will get me a rich guy!'

'And me? Whom do I ask out? I will also ask someone out. I think the Presidency girl was nice. Don't you think so?' Saurav asked, his eyes rolling up and his arms flailing around. 'I think we need more alcohol.'

'We need to get sane and go back home!' Garima said and asked Saurav to calm down.

They spent an hour outside the restaurant before everyone was more or less sane and then got into a cab. Abhijeet and Saurav reached Saurav's place after dropping the girls home.

'You like her?' Saurav asked as he pushed the door open.

'Who?'

'Garima? Who else?'

'Why? Not really.'

'Why not? I think she is fine,' Saurav said.

'Why don't you ask her out?' Abhijeet asked.

'She is not my type.'

'What is your type? Fat? I am sorry . . . I didn't mean to . . . I wasn't referring to Megha.'

'It is fine even if you were! She *was* fat!' Saurav laughed. 'So, Garima?'

'What so? She is not my type either. She is very, you know, intimidating. She speaks less, and though she is good-looking, very good-looking, it doesn't seem like she would ever date anyone like us.'

'I have heard that girls who look intimidating are awesome in bed.'

'Shut up, Saurav.'

'So what are you going to do about it? Are you going to ask her out or something? See, she talked to you first today and she even came out with us. And then, Shruti said you should ask her out! There is surely something going on here.'

'I hardly know her. And besides, do you even think there is a slight chance that she would like anything in me? Also, Shruti was really hammered.'

'Whatever.'

'Yeah. Whatever.'

They slept that day, after Abhijeet reminded him that they had an important training lesson the next day, not paying any heed to Saurav's rants about how much he wanted to see the Presidency girl without her shirt.

That day, they finished their first month in Silverman.

9

The office seemed a blur the next day. They all picked seats near each other; each one was holding his or her head, taking out time in between to look at each other with reddened eyes but with smiles. The video of Saurav and Abhijeet dancing hand in hand was passed among the four of them and laughed at.

They all flopped down on the cafeteria couches as soon as they got their first break and drank their third lime juice since morning.

'Fifteen thousand? Our bill was fifteen thousand,' Shruti said.

'Yes, without the cab fare. Add five hundred more to that,' Abhijeet added.

'That is a lot,' Shruti said again.

'Don't worry,we will pool in and you can pay us back as soon as the next salary comes,' Garima tapped on her shoulder and said. Abhijeet looked at Garima and her eyes told him that she would explain it to him later. That was when Abhijeet realized it was Garima's eyes that drew him to her: big, black, screaming eyes that spoke a thousand words, in a blink.

'Thank you so much! I am so glad you guys invited me. I have never had this much fun EVER,' Shruti said. She had played and replayed a million times in her mind all that had happened the previous night. She finally thought she had a

74

life, beyond parents, household chores, and uninvited verbal and physical abuse.

'The pleasure is all mine,' Saurav said.

'Really? I brought her along. You wanted that Presidency girl. Didn't you?' Garima butted in.

'Later,' he winked.

It was the last day of their month-long training in the training room. After this day, the batch no longer would be together, but rather, under their respective mentors, who were to help them in the initial stages of their career.

Saurav picked a seat near the Presidency girl, but their conversation lasted only a few minutes, after which he came back to where he was sitting.

'What happened?' Shruti asked with concern in her voice.

'Nothing. She has a boyfriend and is in a serious relationship since the last three years.'

'Sorry, Saurav,' Garima said.

'Why?'

'She doesn't have a boyfriend. I know her,' Garima said and laughed.

'Maybe she lied to you,' Saurav argued.

'Yes. Think. Who would she lie to, a harmless girl or a guy who is trying to hit on her. Tough choice, eh?'

'Bitch,' Saurav whispered.

Abhijeet's smile left his face abruptly as the familiar click-clocking sound approached the door. Sumita entered in a saree wrapped tightly around her two-foot-wide figure. As if she wasn't any less menacing, she had chosen a bright red saree, smeared a lump of kohl around her eyes and a pancake of make-up on her face.

'It seems like we finally have some well-dressed adults here. Good.' She continued, 'Anyway, from Monday onwards, you will join your respective departments and mentors, who have been assigned to you according to how you performed during your training. The list has the details and I expect you to go through it.'

As soon as she said this, everyone flipped over the first page and started searching for their names.

Sumita banged the table and shouted out, 'And you *don't* have to look at it now. Not until I leave. For heaven's sake, don't act so childish! Anyway, all the mentors will come to you and will have a talk with you. We will leave you early today and you can spend some time with your mentors after all of them give you their presentations. You can ask them whatever you want to. You can take as much time as you want to. Carry on now.'

She left and everybody exchanged a beaten-down look and sighed.

Abhijeet sank back into his chair as soon as he saw that Garima and he were in different departments. Abhijeet and Shruti were put in Energy, Saurav and Garima got Infrastructure. The Thapar girls and the Sumita guys, those who sucked up to them, got M&A (Mergers and Acquisitions), supposedly the most glamorous department of SF.

The day started and so did the presentations. Every mentor had come prepared with an extensive presentation of how the company grew, how their departments grew and how they grew in the company, occasionally sprinkled with *how-good-I-am-and-was* anecdotes.

Group after group became disheartened, for their mentors weren't what they had pictured them to be. The guys were arrogant and tight ass, but smart and hot nonetheless. Still, each presentataion prepared the four of them well for their mentors, who were scheduled to be the last ones that day.

Quite surprisingly, the supposed mentor of Infrastructure didn't walk in. A guy entered in place of a female mentor and a silent *what-the-fuck* escaped Saurav mouth. This was a gigantic disappointment.

All eyes were now riveted on the guy, not because he was insanely handsome, but because he was exactly the opposite. His hair was ruffled and fell carelessly over his eyebrows. It had been two days since he had shaved and there was a bushy tuft of hair hanging from his chin. He was a little bit on the heavier side, a rarity, shabbily dressed, another rarity, smiling too, catastrophic. I could have gone further about the guy, but let us keep it short.

It was Deb. It was me. It was I (grammatically correct).

~

It had been six months since I had joined the firm and the how and why of that will be answered in due time.

'The person you were expecting will be here shortly,' I said and pulled up my tie.

They weren't expecting me. They were expecting somebody tall and pretty and smart, and I was an anti-climax.

'I guess she is here,' I announced and she walked in.

This time, everybody heard Saurav sigh and pump his fist in the air. Guys who had slouched in their chair sat up straight and fixed their eyes on her. So did the girls. Their eyes had opened wide and mouths even wider. There was an uneasy silence in the room, no one moved, as the girl with the most enchanting smile said 'Hi'.

Yeah, I am going out with the girl with the most enchanting smile, so I am allowed to say these things about her. Not that they are very far from the truth either. She is, after all, a complete knockout. She looked at me and sent my heart aflutter as she always did.

'Hello, everyone. I am Avantika, Infrastructure.'

Avantika, the girl on whom every guy, including Thapar and a few females, had their eyes on.

She was beautiful. Her face was cut along the right lines, as if done precisely by a surgeon. Her lips were pink and full, and her eyes, oh her eyes, could rob you of your soul and send you down a trip to heaven along the thick black hair cascading down her shoulders.

As I always said, it was like a thousand light bulbs lit up her face. I am not saying this because it just happens that I am going out with a girl whose face is almost like a light source, but Avantika is the best-looking girl you will ever see.

The guys were excited to bits at just the sight of her, and I don't blame them for it.

'Hi, I am Deb, Energy.'

I spoke, 'I am sorry but we have no presentations. I asked her to make one, but she spent hours taking a shower today morning. I, obviously, am totally incapable of doing anything worthwhile. Ishita and Ishaan must have told you everything you need to know about everything. If you didn't listen, never mind. It is of no consequence anyway.'

Avantika butted in, 'See, guys. This is a great opportunity for everyone. You know that. This job pays well. Yes, it is a little hectic . . .'

'A *little* hectic?' I interrupted.

'Maybe a lot. But we are being paid for it.'

'Paid? Ask them.' I have always been into office gossip and I knew about the internship programme and the stupid trick the Human Resources had pulled on these kids.

'What? How can they do that?' Avantika said after all the joinees shouted and complained in unison about what Silverman had done.

'They sure can and they did. It's stupid and unfair and if I had another job, I would leave this in protest,' I said and the kids hooted and smiled shyly.

'Deb, how do you know about this internship programme?'

'How do you *not* know, Avantika? The *whole* office is talking about it!' I exclaimed.

'I have better things to do than talk to the whole office.'

I could have come up with something to answer to that, but she looked so cute that I couldn't think of anything witty, and I didn't want her to look bad in front of the class.

'Anyway, class. Just six months. It is a little unfair, but this is what we have chosen to do. So, just stay here and be focused. You will be fine,' she said. She faked sincerity so brilliantly.

'You may lose your hair, have suicidal tendencies, and lose your boyfriends or girlfriends, if you have any. But yes, you will be fine,' I said.

I hated Silverman and made no bones about it. It had been

more than once that I had run into trouble with Sumita and she hated me with all of her blackened heart.

'Don't say that. It isn't that bad.'

'It *is* and you know that,' I argued

'Let them find out for themselves,' Avantika said and rested the case. 'I don't think we have much to say here. But yes, we might not be mentors for all of you but if you need anything, we will always be there. Feel free to ask us anything. Anyway, what did Sumita schedule after this?'

'Time with mentors,' a few students said.

'So who all are under us?'

Four of them raised their hands nervously, and Avantika asked them to meet her at the reception. I looked at the two girls and felt pretty darn lucky.

~

It had been three years that Avantika and I had been together. I had joined the company a year after Avantika, after she had put in a good word for me in Thapar's ears. Thapar was head over heels for her and he wasn't aware that Avantika was dating me. I had been a less than average engineering student at Delhi College of Engineering and that made me an anomaly in Silverman Finance, the mecca of brilliance. I was almost universally hated in office. Firstly, because I joined the company very unceremoniously or through a jack, as they said. And secondly, I was dating Avantika and everyone, at least once, must have cursed Avantika's wretched choice.

Sumita, especially, hated me with all her heart, and would have seen me out of the company long back had I given her just one chance. She took it as her personal failure, having me in the company she so zealously guarded against mediocrity and against people like me—mediocre.

Avantika was more like everybody else in Silverman Finance. She worked her ass off and tried to keep *everyone* happy, not *just* her immediate seniors. But I kept her grounded, sane and emotionally alive, she had once said to me. Silverman was known to suck one's heart out and stuff it with money.

~

Just as we were leaving the office, we heard two female voices behind our back. Shruti and Garima were rushing towards us, while Saurav and Abhijeet followed them.

'Ma'am, we have this assignment to do. The questions are from the training modules and we have to submit it by Monday,' Shruti said.

'When did they start giving out assignments?' I asked.

'They have, this time. If only you would know something more than office gossip,' Avantika said and smiled at the girls. 'So, you need help?'

'Yes, ma'am,' they echoed.

The guys reached us by then.

'Hmmm, but we are leaving for Pondicherry for the weekend. Just try doing it over the weekend by yourself and we will clear out your doubts on Monday, alright?'

'But ma'am, we have to submit it on Monday,' Abhijeet said.

'I wish I could have helped you but I really have to leave. Deb sir will help you out, okay? He is not as stupid as he looks.'

'What, okay? I can't do this assignment, Avantika! Where are you going?' I asked.

'I have to shop, Deb. There won't be any time tomorrow.'

'So? I am not missing the match for an assignment.'

'It is just a match,' Avantika argued.

'It is the Delhi Daredevils vs Chennai Superkings.'

'Big deal. We are leaving tomorrow and I really have to shop, Deb. Stop acting like a kid and help them.'

'*You* stop acting like a kid. I am not missing the match. End of story.'

The four of them stood there watching us fight for another few minutes before Avantika said, 'Okay . . . I will take the girls along. You take the guys and we will help them out. We can do that, right?'

'Fine.'

'Fine.'

We stomped off and went our own ways. Abhijeet and Saurav followed me outside the building, and we headed to the biggest screen in the whole of Hyderabad.

∼

'Sir . . . this question . . . of the analysis . . .'

'Abhijeet . . . which department?'

'Sir . . . Energy.'

'Who else is in Energy?'

'Shruti.'

'Same assignment?'

'Yes, sir.'

'Copy it.'

'What?' Abhijeet asked as if it was a sin to do so.

'And I do it from Garima?' Saurav asked, already slamming his laptop down.

'Just change the language. Make sure you do. You wouldn't want to get into trouble with Sumita,' I warned them.

∼

'Argh!' we all shouted in unison as Delhi Daredevils lost another wicket.

'Terrible match. Rohit Kanojia should have hit that . . .'

'And if only Mathew had not wasted those balls,' Saurav added. The post-innings discussion was on.

'Do you guys want to drink something?' I asked.

'I can,' Saurav said.

'Abhijeet?' I asked.

'Hmmm. Okay.'

'Good for me! I anyway don't want to reach home before Avantika does.'

'Why?' they asked.

'She would make me help her in the packing and stuff and that's the last thing I want to do today, especially after this terrible match.'

'You live . . . together?' Abhijeet asked, a little scandalized.

'Half her wardrobe is at my apartment, so, yes, kind of.'

'That is so cool,' Saurav said.

'You bet it is,' I said as we clinked our glasses. 'So? What else about you two? Do you have girlfriends?'

'No,' they echoed.

'Why not?'

'Waiting for the right girl,' Abhijeet said.

'I like the girl from Presidency. The brown-haired one?'

'The one who wears black bras under white shirts?' I asked.

'You know her?'

'No. But it isn't that I am blind,' I answered. 'I keep my eyes open and no one can miss a girl like that.'

'I tried asking her out. But she has a boyfriend, or so she says.'

'Okay. And Abhijeet, what are you looking for in your right girl?'

'I don't know.'

'He likes Garima,' Saurav butted in.

'You do? The girl with frizzy hair and brown eyes? Or the one with the chocolate-brown complexion?'

'Yes, the one with frizzy hair and brown hair. But I don't really *like* like her.'

'He thinks she is scary,' Saurav added.

'What? I thought she was pretty awesome-looking,' I said from what I remembered of Garima.

'I don't think she is scary. Just that she is too, you know, into herself . . . and she snaps back.'

'That way.'

Saurav added, 'In office she is okay, but otherwise, she is all loose jeans, black nails, smoking and drinking, being depressed sort of a deal. He kind of gets intimidated by her. So do I.'

'Tell me about it. Avantika was the same. She was an addict. But that was before I met her. I was petrified before meeting her, you know. Quite like you. Maybe more. I goofed up the first meeting, in possibly the worst manner. But things happened and here we are now.'

'So what did you do?' Abhijeet said.

'Why do you want to know? I thought you didn't like Garima,' Saurav butted in.

'Nothing, really. In her case, all the things that she did were to hide herself from everybody, to run away. She is a very soft person otherwise. Luckily for me, I just found the soft person in her. Maybe it is different for Garima. Maybe not.'

'Maybe not,' Abhijeet said, almost to himself.

We talked for a little while, had a glass of lime juice and headed home. Avantika still hadn't reached home and I feared the time I would have to help her pack.

~

'So, how does it look?' Avantika asked the two girls after she slipped into a miniskirt that was barely there. How could that possibly not look good!

'Very nice,' they echoed.

'Okay. So, we are done now? Garima, can you please check the list?'

'We are done.'

'Good. Let me change. Till then, see if you have any more questions to ask,' she disappeared in the changing room, came out struggling with all the clothes she had tried on, and asked them if they had any more questions. No, they said.

'Coffee?' she asked them.

'Sure,' they echoed.

They found cosy lounge chairs at the Café Coffee Day nearby and ordered their coffee. It was not so much the coffee, as the chairs and the muted yellow lights that got people to come there.

'Will you girls have anything else?' she asked.

'Can we smoke in here?' Garima asked.

'I am afraid not, Garima. You know what, Garima? You remind me of myself when I was your age. Younger, maybe.'

'Why do you say that?'

'I used to smoke a lot and I used to smoke everything I could get my hands on. I have three tattoos from that time. They were really crazy times and I experimented with everything you can experiment with, you know.'

'I am not really getting you,' Garima said, irritated, thinking this would be another one telling her to stop smoking and get her life back on track.

'Why do you smoke?'

'I just like it. There isn't any specific reason.'

'There always is a reason. I smoked because it got me closer to my ex-boyfriend and away from my parents. He smoked because he thought it was cool. Later, he became an addict and so did I.'

'My smoking is not a problem.'

'She thinks, that way she will not have to talk to people since she'd be busy smoking. So, she is probably running away from people, too,' Shruti added.

'See? There is always a reason.'

'Whatever,' Garima looked away.

'Garima, I don't know you. Maybe I am all wrong. Have you heard of Spirit of Living?'

'Huh? The bearded guy who talks in a soft tone and talks about breathing and stuff?'

'Yes. I know you will be cynical but just go to the convention once. Maybe it will help. I am not saying you need any. But it might just make your life a little easier. Shruti, you should go too.'

'Okay, ma'am,' Shruti nodded like a schoolgirl.

'Just try it. There is nothing worse than running away from your fears. It leads to a road that never ends. Just try it.'

'I will see. Can we go now? I really need to smoke.' She got up and left the cafe to smoke outside. Shruti and Avantika looked at each other, blank-faced and concerned about Garima.

10

Shruti had promised to send everything beyond ten thousand rupees home. When she told them about the internship programme, her dad shouted at her for being a selfish liar and wanted to see the circular, and immediately added that she would type out a fake circular.

She disconnected the phone in anger. Her mom called after that and told her how she would be responsible for her father's death, for the sorrow she caused him. She mailed them her internship letter the next day and cried a little.

But things were a little different now. Her mother wasn't in front of her, crying and reminding her of how much they had endured for her well-being, and crying and cursing on the phone wasn't effective enough. She had found a new lease of life, and for the first time, she had friends she could go out shopping and drinking with. She could finally be a normal young person with freedom to experience the little joys of life. Shruti reached office at nine sharp. It was their first day in their respective departments. She left with Abhijeet for the Energy department and started looking for me. They went to my desk, pulled up chairs, sat there and waited for me.

'I am sorry, man,' I said loudly and immediately apologized to people around me as I panted. It was strange that on a floor where a hundred people were working, you could still hear an ant scream. 'I had a TT match which I lost, but I would have won it if I didn't have a sore ankle. Damn it.'

'Good morning, sir,' they both said. I just looked at Shruti and cut out the tall, handsome guy from my retina frame. She smelled good and looked fantabulous. She still looked real and vulnerable, unlike the other women in Silverman Finance who were all vultures with wrinkled skin and piercing eyes.

'Okay then, let us see. What seat have you been allotted?' I unlocked my computer.

Their seats were the fifth and the ninth seats from my cubicle. I gave them their passwords to the computers and directed them to their places.

'Sameer, your manager and the person both of you will report to, is still not here. When he comes, I will introduce you to him. Maybe then you can start working on something important and productive.'

Abhijeet and Shruti reached their seats and logged in. They received two mails from me as soon as they checked their inbox.

The first one said '*Best of luck*'.

The second one had two attachments.

Pinball.exe.
Virtualtennis.exe
Work hard.

When Sameer didn't turn up in the next hour or so, the three of us went down to the TT room, the place I spend most of my time when I am not at my cubicle, pouring over comparative analysis and trying unsuccessfully to make sense out of it.

Meanwhile, Avantika had already assigned the other two some work to keep them busy. It wasn't anything important, but it was something that would help them in the days to come. They had to find some financial data and organize them in a usable way from data sources. The data sources was predominantly Google.

Saurav was a little pissed off with the work assigned and asked Garima to help him out. She snubbed him, but seeing him struggle with sleep in his eyes, she helped him out.

They were halfway through what Avantika had assigned them when Abhijeet and Shruti asked them to join us in the TT room.

~

'I knew you would be here,' Avantika said as she stood at the door of the TT room.

'So?'

'What so? Your manager is here. And he is looking for you. And you two,' she said and looked at Shruti and Abhijeet, 'Rush to your floor. Saurav and Garima, that is for you, too. And Deb, I need to talk to you.'

Avantika waited for them to leave and then looked at me, visibly pissed.

'What happened?'

'What happened? Deb? What are these two doing since morning?'

'Nothing.'

'And why is that?'

'They just joined today. We can give them some time to relax,' I said.

'They can't afford to relax. They are constantly under review. Moreover, they are not you and you need to understand that, Deb.'

'What do you mean they are not me?'

'This job is important to them. You know the backgrounds of these two, Shruti and Abhijeet. It would have been okay had it been Garima or Saurav, but don't misguide the other two. This job is their big opportunity.'

'I am not. What . . .'

'Yes, you are. You didn't even help out with their assignments. What the hell was that? You made them copy it? What were you thinking? You know how Sumita is, right?'

'You are just getting worked up for no reason.'

'Don't act dumb, Deb. You know why I don't want you to screw things up. You know what Sumita wants from you. She made you a mentor because she wants you out of here. You are an eyesore to her and she wants you to screw up. You slip and you are out of here. What on earth will I do here then? And you will take those two down with you. If not for me, at least take it seriously for them.'

She was almost in tears. It wasn't the first time she had asked me to put my act together and act responsible. Seeing me leave the company would not be the prettiest sight for her. For me, either.

~

'Good morning, sir.'

'Where were you?' Sameer asked scornfully.

'Downstairs.'

'Who won?' he winked.

Sameer was twenty-eight and an MBA from IIFT Kolkata. He wasn't very brilliant but was extremely hardworking and terribly efficient. Ever since I had helped win over his wife of two years, we had been *sort of* friends. His wife and I were *good* friends. She often saw who was behind the cute surprises that Sameer occasionally sprang up. In lieu of that, I was spared some office work and shown leniency during reviews.

Abhijeet and Shruti were assigned work and they got busy. While the others worked, Abhijeet was a little distracted. He couldn't stop thinking about Garima's eyes and the story they didn't tell anyone. He called up Saurav to ask whether he should call up Garima. Saurav, quite obviously, said yes. He fiddled and came back and forth on whether he should call her, but finally mustered up the courage.

'Hi, Garima,' Abhijeet said on the intercom.

'Hey.'

'What's up?'

'Working.'

'Nice. Too much work?'

'Not really.' She kept answering nonchalantly and it made him dizzy and doubt whether he should have called her in the first place.

'What else?'

'I am sitting in my cubicle working. Nothing else, Abhijeet.'

'Okay. Carry on. Sorry for disturbing.'

'Bye.' She kept down the phone. Avantika, who was sitting right in the next cubicle, looked at her.

'*What?*' Garima said with her eyes and got back to her computer screen.

Avantika and Garima worked quietly for the next hour or so and it wasn't until Avantika spotted her coming out from the smoking room that Avantika decided to talk to her.

'Any problems, Garima?' she asked.

'No, ma'am,' she said as they both headed towards the lift. No words were exchanged for the next few minutes.

'Ma'am.'

'Yes, Garima?'

'What do those conventions do?'

'Do you want to grab a coffee?' Avantika asked her and they headed for the cafeteria.

'Ma'am.'

'Call me Avantika. I feel like an old hag otherwise. How old am I anyway? Okay, let's not go there.'

'Avantika, I don't know why I am telling you this, but there is no one else I can probably talk to.'

Garima went on to tell Avantika about Karan and an incident that she had kept to herself all these years.

Garima was abused as child, by her own uncle and the memory of that hot day in May, six years ago, gripped her and she recounted the incident to a shocked Avantika.

'I still remember every moment of it. He came to my room ... drunk ... I can still feel his rough hands on me till this day. He grabbed me from behind, my own uncle. I could just scream in silence. I wanted to die, I swear to God I wanted to die, I so wanted to die. He kept violating me. Me? Why me? I had grown up in front of him. Why would he do that to me? I punched him in the face and ran! After that day, I lay in the shower for hours every day and hoped the tears and the water would wash it away. It never happened and I spent the next few years trying to smile through all the pain, fake my happiness through the days. Finally, it was Karan who came to my rescue and things started to look up. I gave that relationship everything I possibly could, but then when that ended, *everything* ended for me. Since then, I have been running, from people, from relationships. I don't want to be alone, but I am too afraid . . .' Tears came streaking down. Avantika hugged her and patted her.

'Before Deb came along, my previous boyfriend asked me to please a friend of his. *Forced*, I think, is the right word, not *asked*, and this happened in front of the whole section,' Avantika said.

'Then what happened? What did you do?'

'I ran and I became you. But surprisingly, I didn't leave my boyfriend. I was too weak and kept enduring the dysfunctional relationship.'

'And?'

'I just stopped one day. The conventions helped, but it is you who has to fight. I fought. And things have never been better. I have Deb now. I can't say he is the best guy in the world, but he is the best for me. He truly loves me. And I love him. I never would have got him had I not trusted him, had I not allowed myself to give in to the temptation to be loved and cared for again. Had I not taken the chance! You are a nice girl, Garima, I know that. You have been through a lot, I know that, too. Somewhere down the line, good things will happen to you. But that is only if you let them happen. You have to let go of the past. There is a whole lifetime to live. Don't lose out on that. Life has been unfair to us and that is why we have all the more reason to make the rest of our lives wonderful.'

Garima just stood there, crying, chipping at her nails and Avantika ran her fingers on her face. 'It will be alright,' she said. 'Let me see that smile first.'

Garima smiled.

'And black doesn't suit you, Garima. Whoever told you that must be blind. Wear pink. We are girls, after all!'

They giggled and went to their floor.

Just as they sat on their seats, Garima looked at Avantika and moved her lips. 'Thank you.'

Avantika smiled at her and got back to work.

Garima picked up the phone and dialled Abhijeet's extension. 'Hi, Abhijeet.'

'Yes.'

'What *yes*? Garima, this side. Don't act all investment banker on me!'

'Oh, yes. Tell me.'

'I am sorry for the last time. I was a little rude. But was kind of stuck in some work and couldn't talk.'

'It is okay.'

'What are we doing tonight?'

'We?'

'The four of us?'

Avantika, who was listening to the conversation, smiled.

They talked for another fifteen minutes and made a plan to leave the office at eleven sharp and have dinner some place nice. Saurav and Shruti were only too glad to agree. Saurav suggested a roadside Punjabi dhaba since they hadn't had good north Indian food in quite a while and the plan was finalized, the first of many to come during that month.

11

Weeks passed and they were hardly seen in office beyond the mandatory eleven o'clock. No matter what happened, they pooled in all their energy in the last few hours to finish the allotted work of whoever was left behind. By Silverman standards, a thirteen-hour day was pretty relaxed and September went past without any hiccups.

The dinner at the dhaba near Banjara Hills was never missed, and it was their high point of the day when they downed their sorrows with glasses of thick lassi.

Every day they dug into piping hot paranthas served with pickle, lassi and dahi, at the only place in Hyderabad where you could get authentic Punjabi fare. The dinners out in the open, on the rickety chairs, brought them out of the drudgery Silverman Finance put them through. That one hour that they spent every day at the dhaba made it all seem bearable. It made them feel alive and it gave them the strength to wake up the following morning.

Sundays were spent at Saurav's place, as none of them wanted to waste time travelling around in the hot sun. Movies were watched, popcorn was popped, beers were clinked, and they still drank like novices and puked and passed out. Those three had started mounting pressure on Garima to stop smoking and it had started to show results. She was down to just a few cigarettes a day. Her clothes got an occasional dash of blue or green and so did the nails. She spoke a lot more now, especially when Abhijeet was around.

Sundays were spent as Sundays should be. Lazily. They called Avantika and me over once, and it was heartening to see four good friends putting everything behind them and getting on with life, staying together and trying to make something more of their lives than what Silverman had to offer.

Abhijeet and Shruti's reason for staying at Silverman had not changed in the last two months, but Garima and Saurav's had.

'I can't leave them,' they both had said once. Adversity makes the best of friends. It had been two months since they had been together, but their bonhomie was unmatched and it looked like they had been childhood friends. Their lives were wretched, their past botched and screwed up, but one thought of hanging out together wiped it all away.

'Hey, Abhijeet. What are you doing?' I asked.

'I was just sending you the profiles, sir and it will just take five more—'

'Leave all that. What about Garima?'

'What, sir?'

'What *what*? When are you asking her out? Are you asking her out? I want details, man.'

'I don't know, sir.'

'See, if you think I am a fool, I am not. Saurav told me all about it. Why didn't you tell me? See, I don't give a shit about work, but if you keep me away from office gossip, we will be in trouble.'

'Sir.'

'Never mind. So when are you asking her out?'

'I don't know, sir.'

'Look, Abhijeet. I am older, so there are a few things that I know better than you. When you get a girl as smashing as Garima, you don't let go. You understand? Especially if that girl likes you too.'

'What?'

'I am not kidding, Abhijeet. Avantika told me this morning. And it is true. So just go ahead and ask her out. She won't say *no*.'

'I will try, sir.'

'Good. And whatever you do, don't let anyone know that I told you this. Right? And I should be the first one to know if she says *yes*. Or even if she says *no*, which she will not.'

'Right, sir.'

I walked away and if I would have had eyes in the back of my head, I would have seen him dancing his legs off.

For Garima, the last few weeks were like a new lease of life. Garima and Avantika went to the Spirit of Living conventions whenever they got time.

'I am so happy to see you smiling,' Avantika said.

'It is all because of them. I now wish I could go back to college and relive the moments, instead of sitting alone in the hostel and brooding.'

'Never mind, Garima. There is a whole lifetime left.'

'I am so glad I found them. I feel so lucky when I am with them and it is like nothing ever happened. And I wouldn't have tried had it not been for you. Thank you, Avantika.'

'C'mon. Leave all that. Did Abhijeet say something?' Avantika asked.

'Naah. I don't think he will. He's too shy!'

'Why don't *you* say something? You like him, don't you?'

'I mean, he is very sweet and good-looking and really nice.' Her cheeks flushed. 'Yeah, yeah. I like him. But I am not going to say anything. Are you sure he likes me?'

'Yes. Deb told me so. And who wouldn't like you?'

'You're too sweet,' Garima said.

'But don't tell anyone I told you that Deb told me that Abhijeet told him that he likes you, right?' Avantika said.

'Right.'

12

'What got you so late today?' Saurav asked. Shruti had stayed late that day in the office and had asked the other three to leave, but Saurav stayed back.

'Nothing.'

'You cancelled today because of nothing?' Saurav joked.

'Saurav, I can't come every evening with you guys. I need to be here no matter how much I hate not being with you guys.'

'What are you talking about?'

'I just . . . I am just a little, well, I am scared, Saurav.'

'*Scared?* Why?'

'I don't want to lose this job,' she whimpered.

'You won't lose this job, Shruti. What are you saying, man? You work hard. Why would you say that?'

'I don't know. People are working really hard around here,' she said.

'Why are you getting so negative about it?'

'Saurav, we are the only ones who leave the office so early. Everyone works or at least pretends to work till their bosses leave. We are the first ones to leave office. Have you seen anybody else do that?'

'But we complete our work. What is the point in staying back?'

'I don't know. I just think we should stay here a little more. Everyone completes his or her work, but they still stay here, just to show the others that they are sincere. More sincere than people like us. I am thinking of doing the same.'

'I think it is a silly thing to do.'

'I know, but even if it helps a little. I don't want to go back to my old life,' she said, her eyes moist.

'You won't have to,' he assured.

'I am sorry, Saurav.'

'I understand, Shruti.'

'Thank you.'

'And I know they won't fire you. Just in case they even think of getting rid of you, don't worry. My father has some connections. He will get you a job. Trust me.'

'*Pakka?*'

'Cross my heart and hope to die. I will not let you go back to wherever you came from. I promise.'

'Thank you.'

'So, what's with Chandni?' Chandni was another colleague whom Saurav had been trying to hit on for many days and was making zero progress.

'Nothing. She says she wants to concentrate on her career and doesn't have time for all this.'

'What bullshit! Why is everybody so concerned about their careers here?'

'Isn't that the fifth girl you have asked out here?'

'Shut up! Why don't *you* be my girlfriend? I think you should be.'

'Yes, why not? We all know what you want in your girlfriend. A couple of months of fun and then you will dump me. Sorry, Saurav. Look some place else.'

He made a sad face and Shruti pulled his cheeks into a smile.

'You will find someone. Who is hot and good in bed and who doesn't mind breaking up.'

They both laughed.

'But will she be better than you? That's the question!'

'Miles and miles ahead of me,' Shruti said. 'Where are the other two?'

'Garima's place, I think.'

'Do you think something can happen between the two of them? After all, Abhijeet is the kind of guy she should go out with.'

'What kind of guy do you want?'

'Rich guy.' They laughed and Saurav reminded her that he was rich and they should start dating each other.

~

Garima and Abhijeet thought about going to the dhaba like every day, but instead, landed up at Garima's flat. It was awkward without Saurav and Shruti around, but slowly they opened up and soon they were completing each other's sentences, even as Abhijeet wondered how Garima still smelled like a fresh morning. He took long, deep breaths and was thinking if his sense of smell would get used to the ridiculously fresh scent and move on, but it didn't.

'You really loved her, didn't you?' Garima asked Abhijeet about Riya.

'Yes, sort of. I mean she was all I thought about then. She was the only real friend I had.' He sighed and looked out at a distance from the veranda they were sitting in. 'You tell me, never thought of going back to him?' he asked.

'A million times.'

'Why didn't you go back?'

'It was easy going back. It was difficult staying away. Never mind, I am almost over it and it doesn't matter now.' She looked away.

'I am sorry I asked,' he said and stood close to her.

'It is okay. There used to be a day when even thinking about him made me cry. But no longer.' She clutched his arm. It sent tingles down his spine and he didn't know how to react apart from involuntarily grinning stupidly and feeling dizzy.

'Goo . . . good to hear that. Listen, there is something I have been meaning to tell you and I don't know whether I should tell you.' He looked into her eyes, and felt like he should shut up, and run back home, and chastise himself because he led himself to believe that there was a chance that he would tell her about how he felt about her and she would smile.

'Go on.' She stared back.

'You . . . have . . . beautiful eyes,' he stuttered.

'Thanks,' she smiled.

'And.'

The harder she stared at him, the greater the tingles he got and the more he stuttered, and the more his confidence shattered.

'Ummm, should we go eat something?'

'Yes, sure.' She let go of his hand and cursed him from within. Abhijeet's head hung low and he followed her into the kitchen. A part of him wanted to curl up and die.

~

The last day of their second month, the four of them were out partying again, despite earnest requests from Shruti to keep from doing so, but then she got drunk and said it was the best night ever.

'What happened yesterday?' Saurav shouted. His voice was barely audible over the roaring speakers of the nightclub.

'Nothing,' Garima said.

'Nothing?' Saurav shouted.

They both entered the smoking area where they could hear each other. Someone offered Garima a smoke and she refused.

'He didn't say it. I think he was about to. But he just kept shut.'

'Did you touch him? Hold his hand? Or something?' he nudged.

'Yes, why? Did he tell you that I did?'

'He gets nervous. Next time, don't do it. Guys like us get nervous when something like that happens, you know.'

'Thanks for the tip,' she said as she darkened her lipstick.

'You have changed.'

'In a good way?'

'You look beautiful now,' Saurav said and Garima blushed.

She was wearing a silver halter that night and Abhijeet had not stopped texting Saurav about how stunning he thought Garima looked.

'But why don't *you* ask Abhijeet out? Everybody knows that you guys love each other. You know that he likes you and he knows that you like him. I don't see why you guys should wait!'

'What? He knows? What!'

'Obviously, he knows.'

'Who told him?'

'Deb told him, I think.'

'But why did he? Didn't anyone tell him not to tell Abhijeet?'

'As if! Didn't Shruti and Avantika tell you that Abhijeet likes you?' Saurav asked.

'But does he know that I know that he knows?'

'Whatever! I'll just be back.'

Saurav went off to pee and they didn't talk about it for the rest of the night. They drank, and smoked, and drank some more, but thought they didn't have enough so drank again, and the next day, they reached office with huge hangovers.

13

Garima and Saurav reached office that day to find Avantika and Dinesh standing at their seats. Dinesh was Garima's and Saurav's manager and Avantika's boss.

'I think and I know that you will be able to work on a deliverable,' he said matter-of-factly to the two new trainees. Dinesh had joined the company a few years back and always had a bothered frown on his face. He was known to give girls a harder time than the guys, and was unpopular in the office. Personally, I hated Dinesh for he was a lecherous bastard. If I had it my way, I would have pushed a rod through his heart for the way he looked at Avantika.

'But, sir, don't you think we should practise a little more before that,' Saurav butted in.

'No, I don't think so,' he said. 'I have given a list of ten companies to Avantika. Take them from her and I want the profiles by tonight. Avantika, you run a quality check on it and then we will send it by tomorrow to the off-shore bankers. Clear?' he asked.

They answered in the affirmative. Avantika nodded and walked away.

Saurav and Garima heard Avantika mutter *bastard* under her breath. They looked at her with blank faces and they didn't know what to make of it. Avantika went to her seat and mailed them the data source and the company names. It was ten in the morning when they started working on the profiles.

Shruti and Abhijeet called them for lunch. They waited till two and then ate without them.

After lunch, Sameer, my boss, was called up by Sumita and asked to give details of whatever Abhijeet and Shruti had been doing. She had the swipe-in times with her, along with the time spent by us in the TT room, and as expected, it didn't mean well for us.

Sameer was given a solid pasting for being irresponsible and unprofessional with the joinees under him. Sumita humiliated him and used the choicest of words for him and for me. She threatened him with consequences, and with increments in sight and recession on the horizon, such threats were the nightmares of many. Sameer somehow pulled through the harsh words and politely took Sumita's leave.

He sat down on his seat and leaned back and took a deep breath.

I let Sameer know that I had assigned work to Shruti and Abhijeet. And also that Sumita was a bloody whore and he should not mind whatever she said.

We had small talk where I mentioned that I knew I was a jerk, and that he deserved none of what Sumita said, and went back to our work in a few minutes.

I checked on the trainees at six in the evening and all four of them were working. They didn't change positions until midnight. The clock struck one. Saurav was waiting for Garima to finish off the work when Dinesh approached Saurav.

'Are you done with what I had asked you to do?'

'Almost, sir. I will just take one more hour.'

'Have you checked the format? This is the wrong one,' Dinesh said as he peered at his computer screen.

'Sir.'

'At least read the guidelines properly. You even had a training lecture on that one. You have read those, haven't you?'

'No, sir. Guidelines?'

'Then how come you are working? I hope you know there is a certain format that every document is presented in. Without it, everything that you do is a waste. I don't know what you were doing during the lectures. Anyway, you know where they are stored on the drive?' Dinesh asked, half-disgusted, half-irritated.

'Sir.'

'Go and ask Avantika. Go through them today. It is not much, just about eighty pages. Go through that and I will mail you some work that has just come up. This is an urgent deliverable and I need it tomorrow morning. I need both you and Garima to start working on this right now.'

'But, sir.'

'Is there any problem?'

'No, sir.'

'Good.' Dinesh walked away.

Dinesh mailed them with instructions, the guidlines and the time by which he expected the work to be mailed to the bankers of Silverman Financial sitting in the US office. It took Saurav and Garima four hours to complete it, and they left the office at five in the morning, exhausted and sleepy.

~

October was traditionally the most hectic month for Silverman, before the holiday lull of November and December, and it was proving to be so. Days were getting hectic with each passing hour and no one slept for more than four hours a day.

Things had worsened. They were just starting out and the only help they got was from us—Avantika and me. Others on the floor had no interest in wasting their time on new trainees who were training to become them. Dinesh was way too condescending to approach. Sameer was better, but he was overworked too.

Garima and Shruti had started getting dark circles and they, too, had gone the Silverman way, or perhaps we should say, the Sumita way, and used dollops of foundation to hide it. Saurav and Abhijeet had stopped taking showers to get that extra sleep time. Alcohol was a strict no-no.

There was a constant look of sadness and depression on their faces from the lack of sleep and the stress that came with it. It was withering them away and they began questioning if they could go on like this. The fun Sundays were over, and they now spent the weekends sleeping in their respective flats, dreading the next week.

Saurav had thought of resigning more than once, but Garima had begged him not to. She would be alone in the department and that was the last thing she wanted. Dinesh was giving them a hard time, but more than that, she hated the way he looked at her and Shruti.

~

'Go to the cafeteria and sleep. Give me your password and I will complete it,' Garima said that day. Saurav had been dozing off in the office and was behind schedule.

'What if Dinesh—?'

'I will manage,' she cut him off.

Saurav nodded and walked away in a daze, without realizing the enormity of the favour she had just extended to him. Saurav had been pushed into working out by the other three and that meant another hour of sleep gone. He was sceptical at first, but the others insisted, and he joined the gym in the office. It was torturous, but he lost six pounds in the first week itself, and started to look thinner, and fitted into trousers better, and hence continued going to the gym.

Saurav walked to the couch like a hungry couch-chomping zombie and fell asleep in a matter in seconds. Two hours later, at around three in the morning, Garima went to the cafeteria and woke him up from his slumber, and told him that his work was done. He couldn't thank her more.

While leaving office, they took the way that went through the parking lot, for Saurav always kept an eye out for new cars that kept adding to the burgeoning SF parking. Garima was waiting at the EXIT gate, while Saurav went around the cars in eights to get a full view.

It had been five minutes when Garima looked back to see no sign of him. He must have crouched to have a look at some customized alloy wheels, she thought. Saurav was a big fan of huge, thick alloy wheels, even when they didn't go with the rest of the car.

She waited for another two minutes, after which she got a little worried and called him up. His phone was unreachable, and she headed for the parking lot. She walked inside the lanes of the dimly lit parking lot, lined with dark cars all along. She was scared now. The darkness was eerie. A light flickered and her heart skipped a beat. It was dead silent, and the clacking of her heels echoed in the parking lot. She was sweating at the brow as she passed a few more cars and saw no sign of anyone there. She took out her cell phone. No network.

Garima contemplated running out of there but she feared something had happened to Saurav. She kept walking, taking measured steps and looking everywhere, clutching her handbag close to her body. She felt somebody looking at her from the darkness. Somebody following her. All the time. She stopped more than once to look around, only to hear shifting steps and the sound of her heels on the floor. She walked into the darkness, further away from the exit. Her steps got smaller. Her breath heavier. Slowly, darkness engulfed her. She reached out for her cell phone again, as she felt an urge to run.

Just as she crossed a black Tavera SUV, she heard feet shifting across the floor behind her. All of a sudden, she felt hands crushing against her stomach and face and pulling her down. She blacked out as the hand gripped her face tightly and pulled her behind the car. The man pinned her to the ground.

She kept struggling and kicking. Her head banged against the door of the SUV, as she kept swinging her head wildly at Saurav, who had blood in his eyes.

'What? What? What the . . .' she shouted, still half-struggling while her face was covered with Saurav's hand.

'Let me explain. I am trying to rape you. Stay down and it will be over.' Her eyes were teary and shouted a *why* at him. She had frozen. Her eyes were now bloodshot and quivering. He came close to her ear and she closed her eyes as tears came down.

'I can't believe you fell for that!' he whispered out loud and smiled at her.

He let her loose.

She cried out and rained blows on him while he ducked and swayed out of her reach. He muffled her again.

'YOU FAT BASTARD!' she shouted under his hand.

'Stop it. Stop it. They will know we are here. I will let you go if you don't shout.'

'WHO? LEAVE ME!'

'Just shut up, okay?' Saurav said.

She bobbed her head vigorously and he left her. She whispered, 'You will pay for this. You could have killed me, for heaven's sake.' She punched him. 'And why are we hiding like this? And who are *they*?' she whispered.

'You will see.'

A familiar face entered the car park from the lobby, and looked around for a car. He checked the keys in his hand and the number plates of the cars. He walked on, passing the car they were standing behind. He kept inspecting the cars till he stopped near an off-white Honda Captiva. The door was open. He looked around and entered the car. And banged the door shut.

The face was Rajat Thapar's.

~

'Why isn't he driving?' Garima said in a hushed tone.

'Because it is not his car, dumbo. He drives an Audi, not a Honda Captiva.'

'What?'

'Shut up.'

Saurav held her hand as they crept up to the car next to the white SUV. It wasn't the best view they could have got but

Garima could make out what Saurav wanted to show her. She could recognize her hair anywhere.

'What the . . .' Garima almost said out loud. 'That girl is *Chandni*? What the hell is she doing with Thapar? What the hell is going on here?'

'How am I supposed to know? It seems like this is her idea of concentrating on her career. She's such a bitch!'

'Shit.'

'Were you following her?'

'No comments,' he whispered. 'I thought she was a lesbian and had come here for Kiran. I thought that was the reason she snubbed me.'

'Kiran?' she asked, with eyes so wide, one could have grabbed her contacts out of them.

'She is in there too, in the car! I crossed the car and saw Kiran and Chandni in the car. I waited for them to make out with each other, but they fucking didn't. That's when I thought maybe something more is up. Now I know, they are here for Thapar.'

'You are not doing that,' Garima said as soon as Saurav fished out his cell phone.

'Yes, I am.' He pushed her back and crept a few steps further till he reached the back windshield of the car. He kept low and raised his hand till the cell phone screen showed all three of them.

What they saw, and what we saw later on video is something we would never forget. From the inside pocket of his jacket, Thapar fetched a small envelope with a grainy white powder, and dropped it on the pull-out tray, and cut lines on it with his credit card, and the three of them snorted two lines of what looked like cocaine. The three of them shook their heads like they were jolted with electricity.

Thapar ran his fingers though the girl's hair as he kissed her. He started to assault Chandni's neck as his hands slipped down to her shirt. He unbuttoned it slowly and took it off. He pushed the lever and the seat flattened to a bed. The girl climbed onto Thapar, pulled her skirt up a little, unhooked her bra and it came off. It was stripped off by Kiran. Kiran was a year senior to Chandni.

While Thapar and Chandni kissed, Kiran had unzipped Thapar's pants and slipped it off. Kiran got naked and helped Chandni to get out of the skirt she wore. They both started working on Thapar as if he had taken a dip in a chocolate fountain and was delectable, while Thapar egged them and grabbed them now and then. Chandni had possibly the most gifted rack in Silverman and Thapar made the most of it. Thapar took turns with them, moaning like a boar, as the car shook and fogged up. Soon, there were too many arms, and too many legs, to make any sense of what was happening. Spent, they lay there, Thapar and the two girls, naked and kissing.

Saurav had got up in between to see what was happening, and he sat down again, his mouth frothing, and cursed himself for being a loser and Chandni for being a slut.

Saurav and Garima rushed out of the parking lot as soon as Garima heard the door lock of the car click.

'Can you believe it?' she clutched his hand and asked. They were still panting and Saurav was on his knees trying to catch his breath.

'Chandni. That bitch. *Concentrate on career*? I told you then, it is all bullshit. SHE IS SUCH A SLUT!'

'Did that really happen?'

'It did. Man!' Saurav was now laughing.

'I mean how? How? And why? What on earth was that? Why would anyone do that? And Kiran? She is a year senior to us, right?'

'I am as clueless as you are.'

'Show me the video,' she grabbed his cell phone.

Within the first few minutes, she handed it back to him, and told him that it was disgusting and she couldn't watch it.

'Did you see them? Bloody nymphets. That bitch, Chandni,' Saurav said.

'What? The way I see it, it is Thapar. These girls wouldn't have offered themselves. Bloody pervert, he would have asked for it. And you, chauvinist pig.'

'Whatever. Thapar is such a lucky bastard!' he exclaimed and started seeing the video again.

'Is there anything we can do about it?'

'Hmmm . . . I don't think so. Not at the risk of screwing our careers and the girls' lives.'

'I never thought I would ever see something like this,' she said and held her head.

'Me too.'

'Chandni? She came here with us.' She shook her head. 'This is so unfair and sick. And we will do nothing about this? Isn't this sexual harassment or something?'

'It will be a huge police case and stuff. And you wouldn't want to get involved. Plus, what if it's consensual?' Saurav wondered.

Garima started to shiver and stagger. Her eyes were rolling and it looked like she would faint.

'Are you okay?'

'Yes, I am fine. It's just that . . . nothing.'

Saurav helped her into the cab.

'Are you going to be okay? Or do I—?' Saurav asked.

'I am fine,' she said.

'Oh, and by the way, there is something that I think you should know. The car they were making out in, the Honda Captiva? It's Dinesh's car,' Saurav said.

Garima buried her head in her palms and the cab drove off.

~

Garima got down from her cab and walked up to her apartment. She was tired and her head was still spinning. The joke that Saurav played on her in the parking lot brought back the most painful of her memories. The helplessness of the girls in the car, the groping of Saurav, and she didn't feel too nice. Garima thought of Shruti, who was helpless and poor and impressionable, and could be driven by a lecherous boss to do what those girls were doing. She called her, but Shruti didn't pick up her phone.

Her phone beeped.

Goodnight. Sleep well. Abhijeet.

Nervous and restless, she called up Abhijeet. She had just started narrating the parking lot incident, when Abhijeet told her that Saurav had already told him. She was crying, and Abhijeet asked her to go to sleep but she told him she wouldn't get any sleep that night.

She was on the phone for an hour, silently sobbing while Abhijeet patiently kept holding on the other side. It was one of those nights when the thoughts of those two days of her life clouded her mind and she felt she would never be herself again. A little later, she told a shocked Abhijeet about how she was molested, and Abhijeet, furious and full of questions, took a cab and reached her place in an hour.

The minute she saw Abhijeet standing at the doorstep, his eyebrows making a small hill on his forehead and his fists clenched, she felt calmer. They hugged and she counted seconds uptil which she could keep resting her face on his chest and it wouldn't be awkward. She felt safe.

'Will you have something?' Garima asked him.

'Have you had anything?' he looked at her and asked. She smiled and shook her head.

'Never mind. I will make you something good to eat.'

'You can cook?'

'Of course I can cook. I used to cook a lot in my college days,' he said, his face contorted as if he felt insulted.

'So what are you making for me today, chef?'

'It is a very easy thing to make. But it tastes like heaven,' he said as he rummaged through her kitchen. 'It is probably French but I make an Indian version. It's spicy and works well with ketchup. Just wait.'

'So, what is it?'

'You might have heard about it. It is very popularly known as *Maggi*.'

'Ugh! LOSER!' she said out loud and started to hit him playfully. They got into a cute little mock fight, which ended when she felt like grabbing him and thrusting her lips onto his. She stepped back and blushed.

'Okay, I will sit here while you cook,' she said and climbed up the slab, right next to the stove.

He proceeded to crush the cakes into small pieces and added them to the steaming water. All this time, Garima sat there, looking at him, as he did very carefully what people could do with their eyes closed. It took ten minutes for the noodles to cook, and he slathered it with ketchup, and he served it in the utensil he cooked it in.

'You are sweet.'

'I know,' he said as he rolled a noodle around a fork and made her eat it.

He told her that he was full and made her finish the Maggi, and found an apple in the fridge for her to eat. She didn't want to talk about the incident in the parking lot, or her past, and she just talked about how much they missed Delhi and their parents. She talked endlessly, and Abhijeet listened patiently.

After that, he led her into her bedroom and tucked her inside. She had already started missing him. She remembered the last time he had left. It had seemed like her flat's walls had exploded, that it had grown twice in size, and it was a huge empty space, and she felt lonely and alone.

As soon as he left the bedroom and was about to disappear behind the door, she said, 'Please stay.'

'But.'

'Sorry, you can go.'

'I will stay.'

He bolted the door and sat on the bed next to her. She put her arms around him and her eyes welled up, and she barely suppressed an urge to tell him that she never wanted him to go out of her sight.

'Thanks for staying.' Garima clutched his hand and kept her head on his shoulder.

'I wanted to stay. I like your flat better than mine. It is so much nicer and smells like you.'

She smiled. She grabbed his hand and put it across her shoulder and asked him, 'Is there anything that you wanted to say?'

'What? Me? No. I don't think so,' he said, shocked.

'Saurav told me.'

'What, what? What did he tell you?'

'That, you know, that you like me,' she purred.

'He is such a . . .'

'You didn't want me to know?'

'No, I did, but not like this. It would have been better had I told you.'

'So, you have your chance today. You already know what I am going to say, so you can stop being nervous and tell me whatever you want to.'

'You are the best thing that has ever happened to me, Garima.'

'Go on. Just one line? No wonder you have been single all your life,' she said and punched his arm.

'I don't know what to say.'

'Then find something to say.'

'I don't know, Garima. The thing is, I really like you. I don't know what to call this, but I feel I can be myself in front of you. Awkward, geeky and with no social skills. I know it's been just a little while but I have never felt so comfortable around anyone. This seems natural. I love you, I think?'

'See? You found something so sweet to say.'

'Not really the response I was looking for.'

'Aww . . . I love you, too. I think?' She pulled him near and pecked him.

'Thank you, but not really the kiss I was looking for either,' he smirked.

'Is it so?' she smirked back.

She bent over and he pulled her over him. Her lips touched his and they kissed, exploring each other as if to make up for all the time they hadn't kissed. His hands ran through her fuzzy hair, her flawless skin. She grabbed his hair and pulled at them. The kiss lasted till they were out of breath and they parted and started to smile, and then laughed. Many more small kisses followed thereafter. Abhijeet was hooked to her honey-sweet lips.

Abhijeet pumped his fist and said, 'First kiss.'

'How mean!'

'You should be happy it is with you,' he said.

'With Riya?'

'That was just a peck and it was just because I had done her assignment.'

'Okay. And it wasn't bad for the first time. Come here. Let's try it again,' she said. They kissed again.

The mention of Riya and *first kiss* brought back memories for both of them. Memories they would rather forget. They spent the day in each other's arms, thinking that this would be a new beginning.

14

'Yes, Thapar,' Sumita said as she entered his room.

'Things are looking down,' he said. Thapar's tone never showed the urgency of any situation, breezing through entire life-changing discussions as if he was deciding what to eat for lunch.

'I heard there were discussions in the US office. Did they call?'

'Yes. The subprime thing has really started to hit. Too early to say, but pundits fear the worst. We need to be prepared.'

'What is the worst?'

'We are looking at halving the workforce and it could happen overnight.'

'Are you serious?' Sumita was sweating now. She pulled up a chair to sit.

'They can kick us out, too. You and me.'

'What? Why me?'

'We are extra staff, Sumita.'

'What do you mean? I have upheld the values of the firm for so long. They can't do that to me. I am the Head HR.' For probably the first time, Sumita had gone soft, and she was nervous.

'Don't worry yet, Sumita. There is still time.'

'When should I start worrying?'

'Pretty soon. If we don't show them performance, we are cooked. Half of us will be gone for sure.'

'What? Half the staff is working nights. How can we kick them out? You can't expect to halve the workforce and still get work done.'

'I don't care how you get work done. Show me some figures. I want the charts to go up. Bring up managers, threaten them with life. Make it work. I want man-hours, quality man-hours. And if that does not happen, well . . .'

'Then?'

'Anything can happen.'

~

Earlier that month in Shri Ram College of Commerce, New Delhi.

'Are you okay working nights?' the interviewer asked.

'Yes, sir, certainly,' she said with a sincere nod.

'The schedule may go into days on end.'

'I have no problem, sir. This is how I will learn. I am a very hard worker.' She gave him a disarming smile.

'Are you sure?'

'Yes sir.'

'You will be able to live alone? And the stipend will hardly cover your living expenses in Hyderabad. You would have come to know about that by now,' the interviewer said.

'Yes, sir. But that won't be a problem. I can make friends quite easily, I am sure I will be able to manage it. Besides, I have some friends in Hyderabad.'

'Oh, you do?'

'Yes, sir,' she said.

'And where do they work?' he asked.

'One of them works in this very company. Silverman Finance. He was a great friend of mine, my senior, Abhijeet. I don't know if you know him. He is tall, fair and wears spectacles. No, I guess he had started . . .'

'Okay, okay! I get it. Seems like it is time to meet that friend of yours. Welcome to Silverman Finance. You will get your formal acceptance for the internship in a while. Congratulations, Riya. I like your spunk.'

The interviewer, Udit, a known pervert, had taken the interview, shaken her hand and smiled at her.

It had been six months since she had broken up with Arjun. More precisely, Arjun had dumped her when Riya took a stand on not sleeping with him, and Arjun had thrown a fit and called her a retrogressive bitch. Since then, she had concentrated on her studies as she couldn't bear the sight or thought of Arjun any more. That meant no more movies with friends. Or night-outs. However, she still wore pink, slightly muted shades, though. Not to mention, her new peer group in college—the geeks—got a makeover, thanks to her.

All the hard work had paid off. She had bagged the coveted internship at Silverman Finance, along with a few others, and she was happy about that. Although she dreaded meeting Abhijeet again, she knew she had missed him.

~

Shruti was working hard. Everybody knew she was desperately hanging on to the job with all her life. She had not even once expressed displeasure at working so hard, having accepted it as her reality. It was a small price to leave her old life behind and build a new life. She always looked drained, and no matter how hard I or her friends tried to get her off work, she was giving it her all.

Garima and Shruti spent the evening cursing Silverman Finance and all their bosses and super bosses, berating them for their arrogance, and sometimes for the high salaries they drew.

Shruti had bought a pair of platinum earrings that evening. Her first extravagance. She had tagged along with Garima to every jeweller's shop in town, before she got herself those earrings. By the end of the day, all Garima had for Shruti was a string of curses.

'Want to eat something?' Shruti asked Garima as they entered their home.

'Obviously. I am starving.' Shruti whipped up a parantha each and served them.

'Not again,' Garima said.

Shruti was wearing those earrings again, for she wasn't sure if it was worth all the money she had paid for it.

'Don't worry. I am not asking you again,' Shruti laughed. 'What is this?' she asked as she found a card while looking for a newspaper to put her plate on.

'Oh, that? Was just making a card for Abhijeet.'

'Why?'

'Why? Because it is such a good feeling, Shruti. To feel strongly about him, knowing that he feels the same about me.'

'Hmmm, I know,' Shruti said, half lost.

'Thinking of him?'

'Who?'

'Sachin? The guy from your college bookshop?'

'Sort of.'

'Don't worry, Shruti. You will find someone.'

'What if I want him?'

'Then, why don't you look for him?'

'I don't know. I don't know if he even wants me. And somehow, I feel it was never meant to be. At least, we still loved each other when we parted, at least it is a good memory, and it will always be.'

'C'mon. Now don't get all teary. You got yourself new earrings, right? And they look beautiful. And anyway, I told you we will find you a guy, a rich, insanely good-looking guy, someone who will get you new earrings every day, and maybe even that pendant you so liked, right?'

'Right,' Shruti said, her eyes moist, but still smiling.

～

Just before the next day ended, the four of them checked their mails to find what every employee of the IBD division dreaded the most. A personal meeting with Sumita Bhasin. It was sent to all four of them, along with me, Avantika and our managers.

It spelt terror for them, disgust for me, worry for Avantika, and *what the fuck* for the managers. For Saurav and Abhijeet, it was their third call up in three months, and November had just started! All seven of us waited outside her room, Dinesh being the only one who was breathing a little easy.

As my wretched luck would have it, they were called in, just as I went for a leak. Everyone waited, along with Sumita, for me to return. I entered hurriedly and the way she looked at me, I was sure she was trying to make me explode.

Sumita was pouring over some papers, and the very next second, she almost slid them violently to Dinesh and Sameer, the only two who were sitting.

'Terrible,' she said. 'This is unacceptable.'

'I know, ma'am,' Dinesh said. The papers were from the QC, the Quality Check department.

'So? What are you doing about it, Dinesh? Five mistakes on an average? And you, Sameer? No point saying anything to you. Three years and you still don't take anything seriously, do you?' She stood up.

'Let me make something very clear to you. Three years, five years or one. We are not here to cut any slack. You make mistakes, you leave. Do I make myself clear?' She looked at everybody. 'Deb? What will you do if you get fired? These guys may still manage something, but *you*? What will *you* do?' She paused and looked around before she continued, 'And everyone, one more report like this comes, and heads will roll. Now, get out, everybody, and I hope not to see your faces again. I hope I'm making myself very clear here.

'And yes, we have made the shortlist of new joinees who will go to Singapore,' she said. I could see their faces turning red. 'And none of you are going. We are sending fifteen trainees; you are in the other nine. Make sure the nine of you don't fall like nine pins!' She laughed out like only a witch would, her voice shaking the very foundations of the office. She leant forward and stared into Shruti's eyes, which were now red and little wet.

'Shruti, you came real close. I have no qualms telling you

that you were better than the fifteen who have been chosen. But the management thought otherwise, for the kind of company you keep,' she waved her hand around the other three, 'is very disruptive for the company. You can still make amends. The list still needs to be signed by Thapar. Talk to me some time. We will see what we can do. Thapar and I.' She leant back and motioned everyone to leave.

Shruti left the room crying.

Tough times were ahead, and it seemed like Sumita had something planned for Shruti, for sure. Sumita and Thapar.

~

It had been three hours since Shruti hadn't been on her seat. The other three finally found her in the cafeteria, face buried in her palms, crying. The three of them were pushing each other to go talk to her first. The pushing ended with Saurav going first to sit next to her. 'Hi, Shruti.'

The others came and joined them. Their guilt-ridden faces contorted with the pain of seeing her cry.

'I mean, we can stay away from you in the office if you want to,' Abhijeet said, as she looked up, her face smudged with lipstick and kohl and mascara.

'Shruti, we are really sorry,' Garima said. 'We didn't know it would lead to this.'

Shruti looked at them, flicked a few strands of hair out of her eyes and said, 'You really don't get it? Do you? I am finished. I am not getting through this programme and neither are you. But how does it matter to you? Saurav, you are an IITian, you have nothing to fear. You will go back to Delhi to your big cars and your big house. Abhijeet and you can go back to your families, get a job and settle down. What am I supposed to do? *Haan*? You have any idea what I go through every day when I am there? I am locked up. I can't go out and I am made to work in the kitchen, and wash clothes, and every day is like the worst day of my life. You know what? I would have got married by now had I not got this job. They lie nowadays that I am at my grandmother's place. Why? The man I am supposed to get married to doesn't want me to work. And when I lose this, I'll have nothing left. The paan-belching bastard! It doesn't make a difference to my parents if he sleeps with a million prostitutes or treats me like shit. You know why I am doing this job? My parents want the money so that they can stuff his filthy mouth with it. So that there is some chance that he doesn't hit me after I become his bed whore. So that he doesn't burn me with his cigarette after he finishes beating me blue. You don't believe he will do that? But you will, when you see his previous wife. Why? Why? Why do my parents still want me to marry him? Because I am nothing but a whore, a prostitute whom they are selling to him. To get my father's sins paid off. Are you still sorry?' She finished, tears streaking down both her cheeks, and went running to the girls' washroom.

While Garima was openly crying, Abhijeet and Saurav's eyes were filling up with unshed tears.

All this time, they had known about how important this job was for Shruti, but the gravity of the situation hadn't hit them until now. They looked at each other, blank-faced. Saurav assured a crying Garima that he would take care of Shruti.

Sumita's outburst had everyone riled up, so while Shruti was in the cafeteria, I was working my ass off. Little did I know what Sumita and Thapar had planned for me the next day, and that my fate was already sealed.

~

The next day, I found my termination letter on my table. It was not a surprise as to how and why it had reached there. I had always expected it to come my way some day, but still, I was overwhelmed by anger and disgust when I saw that letter. I stormed into Thapar's room, for had I gone to Sumita, I would have knocked her down, and bashed her face with a table lamp.

'What the hell is this?' I asked and sent the letter flying into Thapar's face.

'That is it, Deb. Rash behaviour. You are a negative influence. The Human Resources department has given you numerous informal warnings and now they feel they have had enough.'

'What do you mean? I have everything in place, sir. I haven't fucking missed any target ever,' I bellowed.

'It is not about targets. Your style of working does not suit this office.' His calmness about the matter made me want to grab him and throw him headlong out of the window, and then go downstairs and stomp on his limp body.

'What bullshit is that?'

'See, this. Your language, the way you take things so lightly! It is even affecting the kids under you. Have you seen their performance? It's horrendous.'

'But they are doing well under me.'

'Not as well as the ones under Avantika or the other mentors.'

'But, sir. This is just not fair and you know that. I will not take this lying down. I will fuck you up,' I said, now losing my head.

'Deb, I have a meeting. You have to leave. Talk to Sumita if you need any clarifications. And what's more, it's your manager who signed on your termination letter. You can talk to Sameer if you want clarifications.'

I left for I knew it was of no use.

Sameer would have had no choice but to sign on it. The manager's permission to fire anybody was just a sham, and it was a part of the protocol so that the upper management could wash their hands off a firing. Just as I was leaving, Thapar said to me, 'You are lucky, Deb. You have more time than the others to look for a fresh beginning.'

'Whatever.'

I left and slammed the door behind me. Still fuming, I called up Avantika and we met up in the cafeteria. Avantika chided me for being so rude to Thapar and screwing my case further. But then, she kissed me, ran her butter fingers on my face and my mood changed for the better. She assured me that we would be together, come what may, and that I would get a job which would be better than this one. I wasn't in a mood to talk to anyone else in the office before leaving.

I met the security guy on my way out, someone I was often involved in small talk with, and someone who had had his fill from the half-empty vodka bottles that I gave him often enough. He was a friend and I knew it was time for him to pay me back for all the times I used to treat him like one.

~

'I am sure that bastard did this,' Sumita said, as she looked unsuccessfully for any activity in the security tapes in the parking lot. For a few minutes, the security camera videos had gone offline before coming online. In those few minutes, her brand-new CRV windscreen and side mirrors were smashed, the tyres were slashed open, and the word *bitch* was scratched over the bonnet. For finishing touches, the words 'ugly slut' were spray painted all over the car's chassis.

'Where the fuck is the video? Give me that footage, you filthy rat,' she threatened Naresh, the head of security, who had no idea about the missing hour of the footage.

'The videos go to Thapar every day and sometimes he deletesportions of it, citing security reasons. I think you should ask him,' Naresh said.

'Security reasons, my foot! That bastard pervert! But how the hell did Deb know about this?'

'I don't know, ma'am.'

'Of course you know,' she said and stormed off.

Trashing her car with a baseball bat, and then spray painting her car was one of my most exhilarating experiences ever. I wouldn't have given that up even if Sumita came begging to me, giving my job back.

Though, as I had left the parking lot, the prospect of not seeing Avantika every day and seeing her less than usual saddened me. That day, I realized the only reason why I was still there was Avantika. She meant everything to me, and I had always imagined us together.

15

Days after I left the office, Riya joined Silverman Finance as a winter intern, and she looked over her shoulder to spot Abhijeet but could not. She did not think he would talk to her anyway.

Saurav was hanging around the reception, trying to see if Silverman Finance had picked out anyone cute to join their winter internship programme.

Not surprisingly, Riya stood out in her shiny pointed heels, chunky glittery watch, streaked hair and undeniable good looks. Her smile was only too noticeable to miss, and she lit up the place with her beamer. He asked a few people around about her and lost his mind when people told him she was from Shri Ram College of Commerce, and then rushed to the cafeteria to ask Abhijeet if he knew her.

'Abhijeet!' Saurav called out from a distance.

'Yes?'

Saurav pulled him away from Garima and asked him, 'Do you, by any chance, know Riya? Your college junior?'

'Why? Why do you ask?'

Abhijeet didn't remember telling him about Riya. And Garima, for sure, hadn't mentioned her either.

'She is downstairs. At the reception! And God! Is she cute!'

'What? What is she doing here? Did she ask about me? Did she ask about me?'

'And that means you know her?'

For just a second, Abhijeet thought that she had probably come all the way to apologize, but then he realized she had nothing to apologize for.

'Abhijeet? Do you know her? Will you please tell me that?'

'Yes, but why? Did she say anything to you? Why is she here?'

'I didn't talk to her. She is in the batch of new interns who are joining for two months. Will you introduce me to her?'

'No, I can't.'

'Why? Not close enough?'

'No. We were friends, but ...'

'Brilliant! Superb! Old friends' reunion. Please let's go downstairs,' Saurav said and started to pull him towards the lift.

'Please, Saurav, it is of no use. I will not talk to her. I don't want to, and please don't force me to.' He jerked his hand free and walked away, leaving Saurav bewildered.

'What just happened between the two of you?' Garima asked Saurav.

'Nothing. Some old friend of his has joined as an intern, and I just asked him to introduce me, and he got all worked up. You have to see her! She is so cute and hot at the same time! She is wearing pink stilettoes to office. Can you beat that? I wonder how Sumita would react to that,' he said excitedly. 'By the way, where is Shruti?'

'She is at her desk. We are bad company, you see. She will join us for lunch, though. No, but seriously, we have to stay away from Shruti. I can't be the reason for Shruti losing this job.'

'Okay, but you've got to see that girl. I think I am already in love with her!'

'Oh, c'mon! You're in love with every new girl you see, and it lasts till the time the girl doesn't reject you. What was her name?'

'I didn't tell you her name? She is Riya.' He saw Garima's expression change. 'What? You know her?'

'Riya? From Shri Ram College of Commerce?' she asked and he nodded. 'I have heard about her from Abhijeet.'

'When? What? And why don't I know about this?'

'Don't tell Abhijeet that I told you, but they were good friends. Abhijeet had a crush on her, they used to go out a lot, and then they fought and vowed they would never see each other again. They don't talk now.'

'Why didn't he tell me about it?'

'He doesn't like to talk about it. And Saurav, just be a little careful with her. We know what you want from girls, right? So, don't end up doing something that you regret later. I am just saying that they were good friends once. I hope you are getting it.'

'What?'

'I mean . . . C'mon!'

'I am not that shallow, Garima. Thanks anyway. I will take care not to do anything stupid.'

He walked off, taken aback and slightly miffed at how Garima typecasted him even when he had had just one physical relationship, and that, too, not only of his doing.

~

'What the fuck?' Shruti said to herself. There was a surplus in the Energy department and she would have to be shifted to another department. The mail said she would be shifted to Infrastructure from the coming week, and the worst part was that she would have to report to Dinesh, the most unpopular boss amongst female employees, the man in whose car they found Thapar and the two girls.

She re-read the mail for the fifth time. There was no mistake. It was clearly addressed to her. She looked for Abhijeet's name in the mail and it was not there. Only she was being shifted. Was Sumita talking about this shift of department during that meeting? What were Sumita and Thapar planning? Her brain became a battlefield of ideas and it hurt.

'This is so unfair.'

'I know,' Abhijeet said. He felt sorry for her because Shruti had just started showing signs of getting better after that outburst in the canteen. She was working hard, and the other three were maintaining their distance from her in the office.

Sumita's words rang in their heads.

You can still make amends. The list still needs to be signed by Thapar. Talk to me some time. We will see what we can do. Thapar and I.

The four of them sat in the cafeteria, trying to make sense of it all. They knew they were all thinking about what Saurav and Garima saw in the parking lot that day, but nobody went near it. Nobody knew what Sumita, or Thapar, or Dinesh, had in mind, and they feared the worst.

Garima *said* everything would be fine, but Shruti *felt* all her hopes dying inside her. She had already imagined herself and Thapar and Dinesh in the car, naked and writhing, and she felt sick and pukish. She felt as if Thapar and Dinesh had already asked her to meet them in the parking lot. It was as if she had already agreed to it and had steeled herself up for it. Refusing them was not an option for her. *It's not an option, it's not an option*, she kept saying these words inside her head.

'Don't worry, Shruti. Whatever happens, just remember, we are all there for you. I hope you know what I mean. I will talk to my dad and we will get you out of here. You don't have to do anything stupid, okay. We will take care of everything,' Saurav said.

'Shruti, nothing will happen. Just relax. I am sure we are overthinking things,' Garima added.

Refusing them isn't an option, Shruti said in her head.

~

It had been a week since Shruti was working under her new manager, Dinesh, and every day was long-drawn torture. Dinesh was especially harsh on her, and she could feel his eyes on her body every time he talked to her.

'Sir,' she said. The four of them had just met in the cafeteria when Dinesh called out Shruti's name.

'Shruti, can I see you at my seat?' he said and walked away, and Shruti followed him timidly.

'So, I hope you are having no problems in joining our department. The workload is a little on the higher side here, so you might have trouble coping up. Sumita told me that there was a surplus in certain departments and forwarded a few CVs for me to pick from. I picked out yours, so please don't disappoint me.'

'No, sir, not at all.'

'There are these six deals that you need to spread,' he said, his voice a lot softer, his eyes piercing through her white shirt. 'I guess you will be able to do that by tonight.'

'Yes, sir.'

'If there is any problem, you can talk to your friends. Okay?'

'Okay, sir.' She got up and walked to her seat, her head hung low, and sat down, only a glass wall separating her seat from Dinesh's. She could feel streams of disgust pouring out from her body as she adjusted her computer so as to hide from the direct gaze of her new boss. For the rest of the day she worked with her eyes strictly stationed on the computer screen, to avoid any type of eye contact with Dinesh.

She worked hard and fast, just to keep the thoughts of Dinesh and her in the parking lot out of her mind. Unlike Saurav and Garima, who were still halfway through their day's work, Shruti mailed the work that was assigned to her by eight.

'Done for the day?' Dinesh asked her.

'Yes, sir.'

'Going back home?'

'Yes, sir.'

'I can drop you if you want.'

'Sir, I will take the cab.'

'*Arey*, not a big deal. Just let me finish this off and we will go. Okay?'

'Sir. But . . .'

'Why? Is there anything bothering you?' Dinesh asked scornfully. *I had picked you*, his words rung in her head.

'No, sir. Actually I was thinking I will go back home with them,' she said and pointed to Saurav and Garima.

'But they are a long way from over, I suppose. They would take at least a few hours to finish.'

'Sir, I don't mind,' she said coldly.

'Okay, then. Now that you are still in the office, I will assign you some more work. Go to your seat. I will mail you a few more profiles to work on,' he said. All the affection in his voice had dried out. 'I like the fact that you're a workaholic. There is always a choice to make and I hope you always make the right one.'

She resisted the urge to hit him across his face, tell him that he was a jerk, and that she wished he would crash his car and die. She felt disgusted. She felt as if she was already touched by him. Shruti checked her mail and saw that Dinesh had sent her twenty profiles to complete. *Was this the right choice?* She often wondered what wrong she had done to deserve this. She sobbed softly.

Saurav and Garima came to her seat as soon as Dinesh left. They'd overheard the conversation. They looked at her, as she gazed back at them, teary-eyed, and though no words were exchanged, they let her know that they were with her no matter what. That moment defined what they meant for each other and their relationship. They were a family.

They went back to their seats, thanked their stars for the friends they had, recounted the times they had spent together and daydreamed about the times to come.

The days kept getting tougher for Shruti, after the snub she gave Dinesh. She worked nights, right through her toe-curling painful periods. She missed Garima's birthday, so none of them celebrated it.

She clocked eighty-nine hours in the next week, and went home just twice in seven days. What was even worse was that she knew all this would count for naught if she did not give in to what Dinesh and Thapar really wanted from her. What was even more painful was that Dinesh would leave office very early and would not forget to ask how her work was progressing. Dinesh's attitude towards her was getting maniacal by the day, as he kept crushing her under piles of work.

~

Meanwhile, the subprime losses were starting to hit all major banks and economies.

The whole hoopla about subprime losses is simple. You lend money to a gun-toting, tattoo-pierced man to buy a big house, hoping that he will pay you back well in time. Obviously, the man ends up in jail after few months. So there is no way the banks can get the money back.

Take millions of these cases and scores of banks and you will get the picture. The banks weren't getting their money back. The banks lose money; the investors in those banks lose money. The lesser money in the *market*—that is, *in your pocket*—the lesser you spend. The car you meant to buy a few months back will still be standing in the showroom now. So what do the car manufacturers do? Stop producing. What do the workers of the company do? They get laid off!

So, at the end of the day, everybody goes broke and becomes jobless!

16

'Oh yes, Riya. Abhijeet talks a lot about you,' Saurav said. He was toying with the idea of approaching her for the last few days, but he held back, thinking that Abhijeet might agree to introduce him to Riya, but when he didn't, Saurav finally made his move.

'Does he?' Riya asked.

'Oh yes, he surely does.'

'That is nice to hear, sir,' Riya said.

'So, is there a training that you guys are undergoing?' he asked.

'No. They have assigned us mentors and we do some of their work. Basically, getting acquainted with how things work.'

'Nice.'

'Sir, how is the work here? I mean the culture and all. I have heard they have their own stylist here? I asked someone and she didn't know! She, of course didn't even know the s of style, looking at her extra-large handbag and green mascara with red nailpaint. Who does that these days?'

Saurav kept looking at her glossy lips form those words, but not listening to them.

'Sir? Sir?' She waved her hand in his face and broke his stare.

'Huh?'

'Sir?'

'Oh, stylist. Yes, fourth floor to the right. You don't need her, you look fine, in fact you look great!'

'Thank you! That is so sweet of you. No, I just want to meet her once and ask her if she is blind. I mean there are so many girls who wear ballerina shoes with . . .' She went on again. Saurav lost his mind again. 'Saurav? Sir, I really need to go. My boss, Kritika, she is a real bitch! You know her? It is better that you stay away from her. Okay! Bye.'

'Huh? Yeah, bye.' They shook hands and she walked away from him. Saurav had never seen anybody walk so perfectly well on five-inch pumps. Pink pumps. They were a different shade from what he had seen her wearing the day before, and he could think of no one else who could carry them off as well as she did.

~

Abhijeet was neck-deep in work that day. Sameer was disappointed with his team's performance and had decided to make amends. He had buried everybody under him with loads of work, though he had not yet stooped to Dinesh's levels. He was profusely apologetic about the workload and was always the last one to leave the office.

Abhijeet was scrolling through his mailbox when Saurav tapped on his shoulder.

'Look whom have I got?' he said and pointed towards Riya, who was standing right beside him.

'Hi!' she said.

'Ummm . . . Hi,' he said.

'How are you? It's been so long! How are you?' Riya asked.

'I am fine.'

'Thank me, I made the two of you meet. I will get a chair for myself. Will you have anything?' Saurav asked.

'Saurav, I need to go. I have work,' Abhijeet said, his eyes staring coldly at the two of them.

'*Arey*, sit for a while!'

'Saurav, I need to go. NOW,' Abhijeet said and got up.

'You can at least . . .'

'I can't,' he said and left, without looking at Riya even once. Riya looked at Saurav and he looked back at her, confused and sorry. 'He does *not* talk about me, does he?' Riya asked, with little beads of tears in her eyes.

Saurav hung his head and said, 'No, he does not.'

~

A couple of weeks passed before Garima got to know about the incident and she felt bad about it.

'Why did you walk away?' Garima asked Abhijeet who was cooking for Garima that night.

'Did Saurav talk to you about it?'

'Yes, he did,' Garima answered.

'He talks to you? I didn't know he had time for us now that he is such good friends with Riya.'

For the last two weeks—precisely from the time Riya stepped into the office—Saurav had been ignoring the other three. He was keeping out of sight of Abhijeet and was often spotted at the cafeteria with Riya.

'Don't say that.'

'Why shouldn't I? It's been more than a week and I don't think he has been with us.'

'Abhijeet? What is the problem?'

'I don't want to talk about it. By the way, where is Shruti, man? She leaves for home early and doesn't pick up her phone. Dinesh finally decided to let the steam off her?'

'Yes, he has been a little easy on her these days. And don't change the topic.'

'I am not changing the topic. I told you, I am not talking about it,' Abhijeet grumbled.

'You are irritating me.'

'Why the hell are you getting irritated?'

'You feel bad about your friend talking to a friend who talks to an ex-crush of yours. What am I to make of it? Are you jealous?

All I am asking is whether you still have a problem about some other guy talking to her?'

'Saurav is not some other guy.' Abhijeet got up and looked the other way.

'But you have a problem, right?'

'Yes.'

'Fine.' She threw the cushion she was holding on the ground and went to her room, slamming the door behind her.

Abhijeet kept standing there, confused as to how to react to that. Garima had just had a conversation with herself, got pissed, and locked herself in. It was late at night when Abhijeet went to her room and sat where she was sleeping. Her pillow was a little wet with her tears.

He bent over and whispered in her ears, 'I love you. I am sorry.'

'Love you, too.' She opened her eyes. She had been waiting for him to come to her for the last hour. 'But couldn't you have come and said that earlier?'

'I don't care about her. Just that, I don't want her around ...' he paused. 'They can't be together. I mean you know what Saurav wants, and she is silly, she doesn't know where to draw the line.'

'Come here.' She pulled him close and planted a kiss on his lips.

They hugged each other and went off to sleep. Or did not.

~

I had been looking for a job for the last two weeks, but I was not getting anywhere with it.

After days of nothingness, I finally landed myself an interview with an analytics firm where Sameer's wife had worked. I dressed in a sharp, fitted suit for the interview. The slight beard was gotten rid of because Avantika threatened me with consequences if I didn't.

'Why not call everyone home for a party some day?' I said, as I admired myself in the mirror. I wasn't the most super-looking guy, but when you have a girl like Avantika by your side, you tend to think otherwise.

'I don't see them spending much time together. Saurav and Abhijeet have something going on between them. I was thinking of talking to Garima about it, but it always slips my mind.' She came near and smelled me. 'Nice. You will do well.' She pecked me.

'And Shruti? Dinesh still on her case?'

'I am a little worried about her.'

'Why?'

'Dinesh is a bastard and he has let her off the hook all of a sudden. It's a little weird.'

'Guilt pangs?'

'You know that he is not that kind of a guy.'

'Very strange,' I said, as I grabbed Avantika.

'Hmm . . . very,' she said as we kissed. 'Not now . . .'

'Why not?'

'You get through.'

'That is what I am meaning to do,' I said, as I pushed her to the wall.

'Get through the interview and we will make tonight special.'

'Promise?'

'Promise.'

I left for the interview, pumped up and ready to knock down some walls. Sameer's wife was very popular in the firm, it seemed. The interview looked and felt like a mere formality. I was through in a matter of twenty minutes. I was promptly given the offer letter, and it seemed like they had it ready before the interview. I wasn't the smartest or the brainiest guy around. But I knew the right people, and was probably a lucky bastard. The drop in salary was huge, but the perks were aplenty.

Good people. Sleep. Sanity.

17

A few more days passed by and Saurav couldn't stop thinking about Riya, and he knew it was real this time. He knew he was ignoring the other three but he thought he would make up for the lost time when Riya went back to Delhi.

For now, he devoted all his time to leave a lasting impression on Riya. Every day there was some surprise or the other waiting for Riya on her table. Sometimes, it was a new keyring with a cute teddy hanging from it, while on the others, it was a coffee mug with 'Riya' written on it. Soon, her table drawers were full of baubles, trinkets, cards and the like. Riya had started liking Saurav, too, but she was more than a little wary of falling for him. That night, it was their umpteenth dinner date together.

'I really like you. I mean, I have made it a little too obvious, haven't I?'

'Not really. I just have fifty-three gifts and counting? I would have to say, NO!' she giggled.

'Okay, I get it. But you are still to say what you feel about all this? I mean me, us, the whole thing that is going around.'

'I think you're a really nice guy, Saurav. It is just that I don't feel it is right. You know what happened with Abhijeet. And we are still not over it. I mean he is still very angry with me.'

'But that was a long time ago, man! He is happy now and moreover, he is dating now, isn't he? And do you think it is fair? I mean, why should I be the one to carry the burden of his or your past? And, I am sure you will sort it out some day.'

'I hope so.'

'You will.'

'Okay, I think it is getting late. I must go,' Riya said.

'You are not going today.'

'What?'

'You are coming to my place today.'

'Oh, I don't think so. I don't think you're *that* nice. Just kidding, but I really can't.'

'Oh, c'mon!'

'But I can't, maybe we can go some other time. Or we can go out to this really nice place in Banjara where they serve really nice pasta, and we can go shopping tomorrow.'

'I am not forcing you. I am requesting you. Next, I will be begging you.'

'Please don't. I have to go.'

'Now that you are acting extremely stubborn, I will have to tell you, I have planned a big surprise at my place and if you don't come along it will all go waste, and I will be pretty disappointed with that.'

'*What?*'

'Yes, a big surprise.'

'That is not going to work, Saurav. I am going home. You're acting smart with me, aren't you?'

'I swear.'

'Seriously?'

'Yes,' Saurav nodded.

'And I have to come?'

'Yes, obviously. It is for you.'

'It had better be a good one,' she said and smiled at him.

Saurav asked for the cheque and paid it, and then they took a cab for his place and he didn't talk the entire way, instead rubbed his hands in anticipation and in obvious delight. They reached his place and he was unlocking the door, when he said, 'See, I planned it well. If something goes wrong, it would not be because of me, but people who helped me out in this.'

They walked into the flat, and nothing had gone wrong; it was looking exactly the way he wanted it to.

His huge drawing room was bathed in yellow light from the candles placed all across the perimeter of the room. The candles were of multitude of colours and were of different sizes and were kept on different levels. Big thick red candles were on the TV stand where there was no TV now. A table was placed bang in the centre of the room. There was a huge cake on the table waiting alongside a glass trough filled with water, which had green and red floating candles in it.

'Nice. It is so nice. But . . .' she said, covering her mouth in disbelief.

'Yes, go on, you can say nice things about this. I am listening.'

'I really like it! It is so . . . nice and . . . lovely!'

'Thank you.'

'But *why*?'

'Because,' he turned her around and faced her. 'I really love you and some day, I would like to have your life as lit up as this room is right now. I hope to make each day of your life as special as this day is. I hope to make you the happiest you can be, happier than you have ever been. But before I do it, I want to give you something that will remind you of this day,' he said and started to dig in his pocket for something, and after fumbling for a few brief seconds, he fetched a small squarish box.

'DO NOT tell me,' she said and looked heavenwards. 'Please tell me you're not doing this! Please!'

'Miss Riya Sharma, will you some day—if I prove to be a good boyfriend and all that stuff—and we complete very many years of courtship, marry me?' he asked, half bent.

'Are you crazy? Look at that ring, Saurav. I can't take that. It looks so damn expensive. What will I tell my mom? Which one is it? Oh God! It's a Tiffany. But, no! I can't take this!'

'Is that a *yes* or a *no*?'

'NO! I can't take that ring, Saurav. Seriously.'

'Answer THE QUESTION! The ring is not important. I will throw it away right this moment.'

'Oh! What? Okay,' she said, too distracted by the look of the ring. It was a gold ring with a flower-shaped diamond that was at least one carat. 'I mean, yes. I mean, I love you too. I do. I mean, I think I do.'

'That will do,' Saurav said and got up. 'And you have to accept this.'

'I can't.'

'Let us drop this utterly futile discussion about a stupid ring.'

'It is not stupid. It is beautiful!'

'And me?'

'You are so cute. Come here,' she said and wrapped her arms around him.

'The cake,' Saurav muttered.

'The stupid cake,' she said and hugged him tighter.

'It is a chocolate cake.'

'You are my chocolate cake,' she said and kissed him on his cheek.

They always say it is better to be with someone who loves you than to be with someone whom you love. It helps when your boyfriend whips out a gigantic diamond ring to propose to you. If that doesn't work, I don't know what will.

~

Avantika and I entered the plush Taj Banjara Hotel for a quiet dinner, all by ourselves, to celebrate my new job. It had been quite a while since the two of us had gone out for a dinner date and I relished the opportunity to do something couple-like for a change.

We picked a window seat in the café and I told her that she looked beautiful, and then I said this over and over again because I like the way she smiles and thanks me for saying nice things to her.

'You know what?'

'What?' I asked.

'I am jealous of your new job. I wish I could join your firm too,' she conceded.

'You are jealous? Why? It hardly pays.'

'When did you start caring about the money?'

'I don't, but you are so well paid there and the dip is not worth it. You have worked hard for this, Avantika.'

'That is why. I don't want to work hard any more,' Avantika said.

'Very early retirement?'

'I wish.'

'And what do plan to do post-retirement?'

'Stay at home,' she answered.

'Stay at home and do what?' I asked.

'I will let you know that tonight, Mr Deb.' She looked into my eyes as if she would eat me up and I wouldn't have any problem with that.

'Let me know right now about your devious plans. I am so anxious.'

'You wouldn't want a problem in your pants,' she said and moved her fingers up my thigh.

'I would love a problem in my pants,' I said, trying to mimic a sexy tone but failing miserably.

'I would not. Let's order. Keep something for the night,' she said.

'Whatever you say.'

We went through the whole menu to choose what we always ordered, Chicken Lasagne, Mint and Chocolate Oreo shakes and a Penne Arabiatta.

We sat and talked about my new job, about how lucky I was, and how the subprime losses would affect both the companies, and then I got bored and I told her that I wanted to see her naked and she told me that I was the biggest pervert she had ever seen. A little later, food was served and we dug in.

'Shit! I knew this!' Avantika exclaimed as she dropped her fork onto her plate, and looked far into the distance.

'What?' I looked up.

'Look there.'

'Where?'

'There! There!'

'What? *what*? What the fuck? Is she . . .? Oh shit!'

In the distance, we saw what we all had feared. We saw Dinesh walking with a beautiful girl in a short skirt, entering the club that was adjacent to the restaurant we were eating in. The girl, Shruti, disappeared behind the metal detectors, the bouncers, and the intricately patterned gate of the club.

18

Lehman Brothers goes bankrupt.
AIG in deep trouble.
Barclays in deeper trouble.

The news screamed out loud.
All investment banks had taken a hit. Twenty-two thousand employees of Lehman were thrown out in a space of a week. All of them were dollar millionaires.

AIG had cut ten thousand jobs. Citigroup had laid off twenty thousand workers.

Silverman Finance was next.

~

Despite trying hard to keep her feelings in check, Riya couldn't help but reciprocate Saurav's feelings. Saurav had really turned on the charm after the surprise he had given her at his place and she was no longer wary of acting as his girlfriend. Earlier, she had avoided talking to him in the office for the simple reason that Abhijeet might spot them, but now, she hardly thought twice before hugging him.

Abhijeet had noticed them more than once. He felt his stomach churn whenever he saw the two of them together. It had been almost a month that he and Saurav had talked and it didn't seem like they would again any time soon.

Abhijeet and Garima chose a different seat from where Saurav and Riya were sitting. Shruti was nowhere to be seen. She was probably working. They had started noticing that Shruti and Dinesh left for home within a few minutes of one another every day. Abhijeet had followed her once but he saw her getting into the cab she always went home in. *Maybe they meet somewhere else*, they thought. Abhi and Garima were disgusted with her behaviour, and they often thought of asking her, but after her cafeteria outburst, they didn't have the courage. It was her life after all and she had the right to make her own decisions.

Everyone was eating peacefully at the cafeteria when the volume of the TV set was turned on loud. Everybody looked up to see what was happening. A nice-looking female on Headlines Today was reading out the Breaking News from a teleprompter.

Close on the heels of banking giant Citibank's decision to eliminate around 20,000 jobs worldwide, Silverman Finance is reported to be planning to cut around 10,000 jobs from its investment banking business in the coming weeks.

Silverman Finance is planning a reduction of 10,000 staff in the coming weeks, mostly from its global banking and markets workforce that spans around 50 countries, including India.

It said that jobs were likely to be cut in the city of Hyderabad, adding that Silverman Finance's high street operations and that of its subsidiary Natwon would remain unaffected. Silverman Finance employs around 1.7 lakh people, of which around a 4,000 are in India.

The newspaper also reported that Silverman Finance would cut around 15 per cent of its global banking and markets work force, while saying that the move would not affect employees from the US, and would mainly centre on Silverman Finance's investment banking arm.

The report of planned job cuts ...

There was pin-drop silence in the room for the next few minutes, the room turned cold and conversations stopped. An uneasy silence gripped the room. Every look turned into a stare. The feeling of who will be sacked and who will stay, gripped everyone.

Everybody in Silverman Finance may have done a million things, but out of those, one thing was common—they had cribbed about their job. But now, everyone realized how much they loved their job. One in every two employees would go, lose his or her job, lose the life he or she was accustomed to.

Thapar had been right that I was lucky, and I had had more time than others to look for a job. And less competition.

Within the next few minutes, a meeting of IBD was called.

Thereafter, Thapar gave an awful speech about how things would be fine and left no impact whatsoever on anyone who was listening in. The tension and anticipation was palpable. The respect now shown to Sumita was seen to be believed. Everyone who saw her didn't forget to tell her how young she looked or how pleased they were to talk to her. They believed, if anyone could save them from being sacked, it was her.

19

'I don't know,' Abhijeet said. 'If they throw us out, which they probably will, I have no idea what I will do.'

Garima had called up Saurav and Shruti and had forced them to take time off for this night at Abhijeet's place. They were all there, but there were hardly any words exchanged before Garima asked this question.

'Nothing will happen. It will do us no good to think about it,' Garima said.

'Saurav will go to Delhi, of course.' Abhijeet said sarcastically. 'So will you,' he looked at Garima and said.

'Whatever,' Saurav said as he sipped his beer.

'I can't go back,' Shruti said.

Abhijeet and Garima exchanged a wry expression, for they knew that she had kept her manager in her pocket, however she might have done it. Dinesh would make sure Shruti stayed.

'You don't need to go back to Delhi, Shruti. Dinesh would do anything to keep you in the company,' Abhijeet said.

'What?'

'Nothing.'

'Why are you saying that?' she asked, perplexed.

'You know why. I am not talking about this.'

'No, tell me,' she demanded.

'You know it, Shruti. Deb sir saw you with Dinesh at the Taj. You were entering a club with him. What do we make of that?'

'What?' Saurav butted in, shocked.

'Yes, so?' Shruti asked.

'Is it true?' Saurav asked.

'Yes,' Abhijeet said. 'And leaving with him every day? Every single day you left within minutes of him leaving the office. What's up with that? Do you think we didn't notice that?'

'So what? Don't you go out with Garima? And Saurav and that new intern, Riya? If you can go out, then why not me? It has been a month since we hung out together. Every one of you was busy. Why should I be alone? Why should I be the one sitting at home and waiting for the three of you to at least pick up my calls? But no, you are either with Garima, Saurav with Riya or your phones are busy. You guys don't even call back.'

'We were just a little caught up and busy,' Garima clarified.

'Garima, you were so busy that Abhijeet stayed over at your place night after night. And Saurav, when was the last time you came to my seat? I don't even want to talk about it. I just don't. Anyway, Dinesh is not as bad as we thought him to be. He helped me. And he helped you, too.'

'Helped us? What the fuck do you mean?' Saurav bellowed.

'Don't swear, Saurav. I requested him to keep the load down on us. Can't you see it? I asked him as a friend and he did it.'

'I don't want the load to be down if it had be in that way. And you call him a *friend*?'

'Saurav, I think you are blowing it out of proportion.'

'Whatever you might say, Shruti. We are concerned about you. We don't want you to—' Abhijeet stopped short.

'What is wrong with you?' Shruti asked, irritated.

'What is wrong with *us*? You are bloody sleeping with your bastard boss, that's what's wrong with us,' Saurav said.

'For heaven sake!' Shruti threw her hands in the air and got up. 'You really think so? We are just friends. *Just friends.* Do you get that?'

Saurav was already pacing around the room, angry and flailing his hands in the air. He said, 'Friends? Friends who sleep together? You hated him and now you call him your friend? What do you do with him? Play chess? I don't think so! We all know what happens in the car park. We have seen it. We all have. I told you I would get you a job. I fucking told you. You didn't have to go to him.'

'Could you have asked me at least?' Shruti said. 'How the hell did you even think!'

'What is there to ask? You fucking went out with him! I don't care whether you slept with him or not. But you fucking hated him! So now ... *why*? And you call *him* a *friend*. What are *we*?' Abhijeet shouted and looked at Saurav whose face had flushed red with anger.

Saurav picked up Abhijeet's line of questioning. 'I think you really deserve what you are getting, Shruti. The bastard in Delhi you are going to marry. I pity that guy. He should have known better. What the fuck, Shruti? You have let me down ... you have let us down ... You are so ... I don't want to see your face ever again. Leave this room right now. You have fucking insulted me. Us all. You know what he put us through. And what? You called him a friend? A friend, Shruti? Why the hell did you have to go and sleep with him? I would have given you all the money. I would have, man ... just go to hell. It is all about the money, isn't it? Everything for you ... you should have asked me, just once ... *Dinesh?* Everything is about you, isn't it? Just like your parents said ...'

Shruti looked at the three of them, shocked and in disbelief, and then her eyes started to well up, and then she tried to look for words to defend herself but she couldn't find any. She was hurt, not because she couldn't defend herself and make them understand but because her friends could accuse her of sleeping with Dinesh. And what if she had? Dinesh was around when none of her friends were. Did that mean they would abandon her?

'I had no other choice,' she said and left the house, banging the door behind her.

'You always have a choice,' Abhijeet said as she left.

Silence gripped the room. Everybody looked at each other, as if to ask the question whether they had gone a little too far.

Abhijeet thought he had not. The very fact that she met their most hated guy outside office angered him beyond limits. Garima was still angry but not so much. Saurav was too dazed to think anything. Only if they had thought about things from her perspective. Only if they had realized that they had left her alone.

'Did we say too much?' Garima asked.

'No,' Saurav said.

'I think so. Saurav said too much,' Abhijeet said.

'I said too much? Are you crazy? And why the hell didn't you guys tell me about this before? Why didn't I know about Dinesh and Shruti?' Saurav asked.

'If only you had had time out for us, away from that girlfriend of yours.'

'Her name is Riya.'

'Whatever her name is, I don't care,' Abhijeet said and got up. 'The bottomline is that you are the one who fucking said too much. That, too, when you hardly knew anything. You think you are very smart because you could land a girl I couldn't, impressing her with all that money and stupid gifts of yours.'

'Don't act childish.'

'Will you fight with me for that girl of yours? That fucking little girl of yours?'

'She is Riya. Her name is Riya.'

'I know what she is. I know her. And I know what kind of a girl she is.'

'What the fuck do you mean?'

'What? You wanted a girl to have fun with, and you get a girl exactly like that. Good for you, Saurav, because I have heard she has a lot of experience!'

'I know everything about her.'

'You know shit about her,' Abhijeet said as his temper peaked. 'Ask her what all she did with Arjun. All that guy had to do was to ask and she was there for him.'

'Shut up, Abhijeet, you are sick and need to shut up right now.'

'What sick? Ask her.'

'For God's sake! He was her boyfriend.'

'So what is the fucking difference? Why the double standards? Shruti slept with Dinesh to keep her job safe and that is so *not* acceptable to you, but when your girl sleeps with her awesomely rich boyfriend just to keep him from going away, that is acceptable?'

'*What the hell?* She did *not* sleep with him. And even if she did, I don't give a damn.'

'Guys!' Garima shouted to keep them from shouting.

'No, let him speak, Garima. I didn't know Abhijeet could say such nice things about his friends. Maybe tomorrow he will say the same about you and me and everyone he is friends with today!'

'Friends, my foot! She is not my friend. Never was. She doesn't even know what friendship is. That bitch! And how dare you fucking say anything about Garima.'

'You are such a bastard, Abhijeet,' he grumbled.

'Fuck off, man! You will come to know when she leaves you some day and we won't be here.'

'She won't leave me and you need to shut that fucking mouth of yours or I am going to fuck you up,' Saurav said and turned around to leave.

'I wish she does leave you. And where are you going? Oh, to her? Don't forget to fuck her. She will be ready to do it. Just tell her you will dump her otherwise.'

Saurav turned back and rushed towards Abhijeet and rammed his head onto Abhijeet's chest. Abhijeet staggered and moved backwards towards the wall, stepped on a glass which broke beneath his feet and banged his head on the wall. He fell on the ground and immediately a pool of blood formed where his head lay.

'That is what you deserve, bastard,' Saurav said as he looked down at him. The very next second he realized that Abhijeet was hurt. As he bent to see the damage, he was slapped hard by Garima, who was now in tears.

'Get the hell away from him!'

'But!'

'Just go away,' she wailed out loud and bent down on Abhijeet who had almost blanked out.

'Ga—'

'Get out! Get *out*!' She stood up and grabbed Saurav by his hand. 'Get the hell out of my house and don't come back here again.' She pushed him outside the door and shouted, 'Don't ever come near him or me. Ever again.' She banged the door on his face and went back to see Abhijeet. He was helping himself up against the wall, his head smashed and glass pieces lodged inside the bottom of his feet.

Garima kept herself from fainting, seeing all the blood around. Her stomach churned to see the glass pieces sticking out of Abhijeet's feet.

It took half an hour for the paramedics to arrive. Till then, Garima cradled Abhijeet's head—which was no longer bleeding in spite of a deep wound—and kept crying.

Neither the shattered glass nor the wound hurt as much as . . . their shattered family.

~

Abhijeet spent the next day in hospital. There were thirteen stitches on his feet and four on his head. A bandage was wrapped around his head like a bandana and he was asked not to keep his foot down for the next week or so. Neither Saurav nor Shruti asked how Abhijeet was, or visited the hospital. Dinesh had texted though and wished for a speedy recovery. Sameer, Avantika and I had gone to visit him to see how he was.

Garima also took off for the next two days, but came back to the office on the third. Whenever Garima saw Dinesh now, she had an uncontrollable urge to snuff the life out of him.

Finally, on the fourth day, Abhijeet had recovered enough to join office. He was limping on one foot, and had a hockey stick in hand. Sameer had asked him to stay at home but he would not listen. It was partly because his job was on the line and mostly because Garima had once called from office and cried because she had no one else to talk to. She had filled up Abhijeet's inbox with mails about how much she missed him. Abhijeet told her that if they were to lose this job, they would do it together.

The four of them did not meet that day.

They took different seats in the cafeteria.

Abhijeet and Garima sat in one corner. Saurav sat in one with Riya, who was crying softly. Shruti was in another with the team. Sometimes, they exchanged glances but when they saw the other person looking their way, they turned away. Everybody had found people to bitch about the others.

~

'I don't want to talk about them. Can we talk about something else?' Shruti asked. This was her fourth conversation with the Silverman Finanace guy who lived next door. He was a few years senior to her and although he had tried asking her out a couple of time, Shruti had played smart and found a way to wriggle out of it. That day, Shruti was home earlier than usual and the guy, Rahul, invited himself over. Since she was bored and depressed and lost, she thought she could do with some company for a while.

'No please. You've got to tell me.'

'Why do you want to know?'

'I don't want to. I need to know,' he tried the sympathy card.

'Why?'

'Because I need to know what is bothering you so much,' the guy said.

'Nothing. It is just that they thought I was sleeping with my boss. All I wanted to do was help myself. And they didn't even bother to ask how I was doing ... all those months!'

'Maybe you should have talked to them.'

'What *talk to them*? I don't need to tell them everything. And I don't need to tell you everything.'

'Why don't you talk to them now?'

'That chapter is over. Forever. I don't want to talk to them ever. Let's talk about something else.'

'Okay.'

She dozed off twenty minutes later. Rahul could do nothing but depress her further. She saw him leave the room. Then, she got up and wrecked the room, throwing everything around and shouting out loud before she sank on the floor and cried the night away. She stared at the kitchen and the knife that was there . . .

It wasn't over yet. She cried a little more.

~

Abhijeet and Garima had tried to avoid talking about Saurav or Shruti, following that day.

'You have nothing to say?' Garima asked.

'About?'

'About that day and what happened.'

'No.'

They stayed silent for a while, and then Abhijeet said, 'It is Saurav's birthday today.'

'I know,' Garima said. 'I don't think we are wishing him. I am not. After what he did to you, he didn't even have the decency to at least come and see you once.'

'Okay.'

'No, I am serious, Abhijeet. He saw what happened. You were bleeding from everywhere and it is not like he doesn't know. And that friend of yours, Riya, she didn't even think once to ask how you were doing.'

'Even Shruti didn't, but I think we said a little too much. But she didn't do the right thing. I mean, it is unimaginable . . .'

'I do not know. That was the last day I talked to them. I so hate them. It's not as if they don't matter to me. They do. And that is why I hate them more,' Garima said, as she adjusted Abhijeet's bandage.

'But where is Shruti? I haven't seen her in the office,' Abhijeet asked.

'Maybe Dinesh knows. Who cares?'

~

Saurav spent the night consoling Riya, saying that it was not her fault and that Abhijeet was a selfish, jealous bastard. Not that it made any difference to her or her crying, but it made Saurav hate Abhijeet even more with every passing second that she spent crying. He didn't like the fact that Riya was crying because of him. Moreover, he knew that he would have to choose between her and Abhijeet. And a million times over, he would choose Riya.

The buzz about layoffs was gaining ground as days passed by. It was now official; half the teams would go. People who had eternally hated their jobs with all their heart were now mortally scared.

Some of the new joinees had started looking for new houses. Small, affordable ones. Many had updated their CVs and had started forwarding it to their friends in lesser organizations who were having a field day seeing these overpaid pigs suffer. Everyone applied for premium accounts on job-hunting websites and stared at the inboxes, waiting for interview calls.

Tragedy brings people closer and this was happening in Silverman Finance long before it actually struck. People who sat in adjacent cabins but never talked were now talking about everything from which schools their children went to and whether they had applied to any place else, just in case they lost this job.

Nobody had anything else to do in those fifteen days.

Abhijeet had panicked and freaked out, after reading the official announcement of the layoffs, but Garima said he could join her father's business if he wanted to. Garima had already told her parents about Abhijeet and they were only too happy to hear their daughter sound happy again.

And to think of it, losing the job was no longer that bad an option for him. He had his life set, a business of his own. Having a rich girlfriend helps. Abhijeet now had one . . . just like he had once mentioned to Saurav that he had wanted one.

20

It was the first time that she was doing this. And it wasn't Delhi or Chandigarh where there were alcohol shops in malls and in markets right next to convenience stores. The people jostling for bottles were rickshaw pullers and labourers, half of whom had forgotten what they had ordered when they saw her approaching. She pulled down her T-shirt and tried to be extremely loud and confident.

'Smirnoff vodka. Two. Full.' She took out her cell phone and yakked loudly. '*Haan*, bring the car around. Ask Amit and Rajat to come. Make it quick, man.' She then went ahead and ordered five beers, too. It lent more weight to the story that there were three guys coming to join her.

She put them all in her huge red and golden handbag and quickly turned around the corner. She took an autorickshaw and headed home.

A senior had come up to her earlier that day and asked whether it was fun doing it with Dinesh, whether they did it in the parking lot in his car, or he came over to his house. While he walked away, he told Shruti that it was her friend who had told him everything about her and Dinesh. She kept sitting there, open-mouthed, waiting for it to register. She turned towards the computer as tears trickled down her cheek. She could see it in the reflection of her computer screen. A group formed around that guy who had just talked to her and then everyone looked at her and either smiled, smirked or expressed shock. She felt all those eyes on her. As if they were stripping her, there and then, and imagining her with Dinesh.

She had never expected her friends, the friends she had treated and trusted like a family, could indulge is such malicious gossip about her. She clenched her fist till her nails clawed inside her palms.

She prayed for the driver to drive fast. The crowns were peeking from the top of her bag as she clutched on to it tightly. The speed breaker clanged the bottles together and made the driver look at her in the rear mirror. It was a sweating Shruti that he saw.

As soon as she reached the apartment complex's gate, she gave the driver a hundred-rupee note and rushed into her flat.

She missed Saurav. Abhijeet. Garima. She wanted to fight it. She wanted to tell herself she could do without them, and that she didn't need friends like them.

That's when she decided to drink that night. Alone.

She took out the bottles and kept them on the table. She never drank beer. *It is a guys' drink*, Saurav had once told her. Chauvinistic pig, she thought. And wondered why she had not seen that before. He was nothing but a female-bashing asshole. Shruti opened the bottle and the stench made her crook her nose. She held the bottle in both her hands and took a long gulp. She coughed and cringed, while the yellow liquid made its way down her throat, spoiling the taste of her tongue for the rest of the night. She got hold of the bottle again and gulped it down in three huge sips.

She felt nauseous. And tipsy.

Shruti ran over her phone list. She looked for Abhijeet's number. It wasn't in the last dialled numbers. Or received. Nor missed calls. Neither was Saurav's or Garima's.

She found Garima's number in the phone book and pressed the dial button. And cut the phone.

She redialled thrice and then flung it. It hit the skirting of the room. The battery and the keypad spilled out. She had expected Garima to call. She had expected Avantika to call. Nobody did. She wouldn't call either. The two remaining bottles were opened and a glass was filled—half with vodka and the rest with beer. She drank it down. It tasted terrible and it felt terrible. Her throat burned. Her stomach churned, but she felt her troubles dissolve.

She was doing fine. She could do without them. She could sleep with Dinesh. Why should they care? She made herself another one. It burned her insides. She felt hot in her stomach. She felt good in her mind. She was free. She kept smiling incessantly. Thinking of all the times they had spent together. And thinking about how much she hated them now.

With the third drink in, she puked. The next day, she resigned.

21

It had been three days and three nights since Shruti had been drinking. It was the same time after which Abhijeet and Garima had noticed that her table was empty. At first, they didn't think anything of it because it was a day before New Year's Eve and a lot of people had taken a day off. Also, it was already late evening so they thought she might have left early, but then they noticed that everything from the mug which had the photograph of the four of them together to the photo of Shruti with her brother was gone. They looked across the computer and Dinesh knew what they would ask.

'She resigned,' Dinesh said.

'When?'

'It's been three days.'

'Why?' they both asked.

'You should know. She wasn't looking very good and was mumbling something about you guys. I really don't know and she is not picking up my calls. But you should ask her.'

Garima covered her mouth, her eyes open wide in shock, and barely kept from crying. Tears ran down her cheeks and Abhijeet whisked her away.

'We were wrong,' she said, not looking at Abhijeet.

'But why did she resign?' Abhijeet asked.

'Can't you see it? She wanted to show us that we were wrong.'

'I don't think so.'

'Abhijeet, can't you see it?' she shouted. Everyone snapped their heads up at them. She mellowed down and continued, 'We were wrong. Then and even now. Can't you see it? Put your ego aside and open your eyes. Had she been sucking up to Dinesh, she would have done it even now. Why should she leave the job? You know this for a fact that she would die but not give up this job. If she were sleeping with Dinesh, if she were doing it to save this job, she wouldn't have given a shit about our fight and would have still kept this job!'

'Maybe . . .' Abhijeet mumbled trying to process the information.

'Abhijeet! Think. She left because of us! We had each other and Saurav had Riya. She was the only one alone. She was the one who wanted us the most. And we know that she needed the job more than each and every one of us. She was the only one who wasn't tired of getting fucked here day and night. She was the only one who didn't complain. She couldn't have resigned for any other reason.'

'But she doesn't look the type who would?'

'How can you still not see it? Leave it. You don't look the type who would fight with your best friend over a girl,' Garima said, exasperated.

'What the fuck? He was the one who started it.'

'Leave that, I am sorry.'

'So? What do we do now?' Abhijeet asked.

'I don't know, Abhijeet. You and Saurav need to talk to her. Salvage whatever is left, if there is anything left.'

'You go talk to Saurav. I will order a cab and we will go to Shruti's place and talk to her.'

'No, Abhijeet. *You* talk to Saurav. *I* will order a cab.'

'I won't.'

'For heaven's sake, Abhijeet! Will you stop acting selfish now? Put your stupid ego aside and call Saurav up. Look where it got us.' She got up and left to order the cab.

Abhijeet fiddled with the phone for the next ten minutes, as he tried to string together the words. He still did not want to call up Saurav. When he eventually did, images of what had happened that day came rushing back to him. Saurav disconnected the first two calls and answered the third one.

'*Bol,*' Saurav said. He still sounded pissed, though he was relieved to get a call from Abhi after so many days.

'Shruti has resigned.'

'*What?*'

'Yes.'

'So?' Saurav tried to contain his shock.

'Garima says it's because of us.'

'What the fuck? This is bullshit. Why would she resign because of us? . . .'

'I think what Garima is saying is right.'

'Do you?'

'Yes.' Their tones were becoming normal with every sentence they exchanged. 'We are going to her place. Now. Garima has ordered a cab. See you at the main gate.'

'Okay.'

~

On the way to the gate, Saurav went to Dinesh's seat. He turned his chair and looked into his eyes and asked furiously, 'What did you do with her? Tell me or I am going to smash your head into the computer screen. Did you ever ever ever ever touch Shruti?'

'Excuse me?'

'Tell me!' Saurav bellowed.

'Are you nuts or what? She has always been like my sister. She always reminded me of her. I am really sorry for her resignation. She really needed the job. I wanted to help her out,' he mumbled in response to a really angry Saurav.

'How the fuck do you know?'

'She told me. She is a sweet kid. I was thinking of making her the sub-junior analyst. That is why I piled her with work, but it seems like she had more issues at hand.'

'*What?* Then why did you ask her once to leave with you? In your car, the one which Thapar uses? We know about it, sir. Why?'

'That? You got me all wrong, Saurav. We all knew Thapar wanted Shruti. I asked him to leave her for me and he did that as a return favour for all the times he had used my car for . . . whatever. I just wanted Thapar to know that I was with her. I didn't want her to go through what the other girls went through so I told Thapar I wanted her. But it seems like fate had something else decided for her. I am sorry for her.'

'We spotted you at Taj, you and her.'

'She treated me when I broke the news of recommending her for the post of Subjunior Analyst.'

Hearing this, Saurav rushed downstairs, after shouting a loud *thank you* to him and hugging the life out of him.

He came down the stairs and said, 'We were wrong. Dinesh is the good guy.'

They left for Shruti's place and Saurav explained what he knew to the other two, who were now neck-deep in guilt, and thinking how wrong they had been about Shruti and Dinesh.

~

Nobody exchanged a word in car.

They trudged up the stairs to her apartment. Everyone was thinking of what they would say to her. Abhijeet and Saurav wished they were Garima because she was already in tears and they knew she would just sit in front of Shruti and cry her heart out. They were a few feet away and nobody took the lead to go ahead and press the bell.

Garima pushed Abhijeet to go ahead. He fumbled a few steps and walked up the door. The door was slightly ajar. Abhijeet hit the bell and waited. No answer. He hit the bell a few more times and there was still no answer. Abhijeet pushed the door open and a strange putrid stench hit their noses . . . the kind that makes you launch into physical convulsions.

As soon as it reached Saurav's nose, he barged in, half out of reflex and half out of fear, and he looked around in the drawing room for Shruti and couldn't find her. Her phone lay smashed in a corner, and then scared out of his mind, he ran to her bedroom, shouting her name frantically. She wasn't there and the room was unlocked. Fearing the worst, he barged into the washroom. It was empty.

Saurav came back to the living room and they stared at each other, clueless. They stood there for a while, confused what to do next.

Abhijeet and Saurav started to rummage through her stuff to find anything substantial.

They went to the drawing room and noticed the mess, and realized that they had trampled all over the dried remains of Shruti's puke, and there were lots of it. There were neatly stacked bottles of vodka and beer in the corner. The alcohol was too much for just one person. They sat down on the couch and waited for her to return.

'She does have her other phone with her? The one with the Delhi number?' Garima asked, and then frantically dialled her number, but it was switched off. Saurav and Abhijeet searched for the phone in the flat and couldn't find it, and they wanted to believe she had taken the phone along and would switch it on.

Shruti had gone out clubbing with Rahul that night.

22

During the last three days, there was hardly a moment when Shruti wasn't drunk. And though Rahul had not been able to do anything that he intended to do with her, often eliciting abuses from a sloshed Shruti, he was still sticking around, trying for the last day and a half to slip a hand in, or get close to her any which way possible.

That day, they were in Elan, the grandest night club in the whole of Hyderabad. Two of its floors were complete and after the third, it would be the the club with the biggest dance floor in terms of square footage. It was a day before the big bash of New Year's Eve, and the club was brimming with people. It had already sold all the passes for the party on 31 December, touted to be the biggest in Hyderabad, and Shruti remembered reading somewhere about Elan and the man behind the idea.

'Why are so many people here? I think I am still drunk from yesterday,' Shruti shouted. 'Shouldn't they be partying out tomorrow? Rahul!'

'Yes, Shruti?' Rahul said.

'What are your New Year's plans? Where are you partying tomorrow?' she asked and put her head down on the table, not waiting for Rahul to answer.

Blue lights, short skirts and a huge bar—Rahul fancied his chances here. There was so much snogging around that Rahul thought this was the place where he could seduce her into something silly. They sat down on a corner table and she slumped on the table immediately.

'Are you okay?' he shouted above the din.

'I need something to drink,' Shruti answered.

'What will you have?'

'Vodka. Large. With nothing,' she looked at him and laughed aloud. 'Vodka, asshole, *jaldi*.'

'Shruti, don't swear.'

'Don't you think that is cool? Saurav thought it was cool for girls to swear,' she said, as she put her chin on her hand, outstretched on the table.

'I will get your drink.'

Shruti was already drunk and dizzy when they had reached the club, and went off to sleep by the time he got her the drink. He kept the drink on the table and came and sat very close to her, and then put a hand across her shoulder and leaned onto her. She pushed him away as he angled further in.

This happened a few more times, and then finally Rahul, overcome by lust and stupidity, let his hand slip down from her neck and into her T-shirt. It woke her up, just as he was trying to get more comfortable. Shruti leaned away and slapped him right across his face.

'What the fuck?' Rahul shouted and tried to catch hold of her hands, which she was now swaying wildly in the air.

'Stay away from me, you asshole!' she shouted, as he tried to rein her in. The small crowd around their table started looking at them.

'Bitch. Such a slut, you are! You can sleep with that oldie, but not with me. You whore,' he shouted.

'I did *not* sleep with him,' she shouted back and hit him across the face.

'Fuck off. The whole office knows it. He dropped you home once. I saw it. I fucking saw it. And you say you fucking didn't fuck him?'

'NO!'

'You think we are nuts? You used to work late and now you leave office by eight. Do you think we are all fools? Everyone suspected it, bitch. It was a matter of time. The day I talked about you in the office, your game was over, bitch.'

'*You* told everyone? YOU?' She opened her eyes and pointed her finger at him. 'I told you that I didn't sleep with him!'

'And you think I will believe a whore like you. I saw you in his car . . .'

At this point, Shruti put her head down and started sobbing. A few painful minutes passed. Rahul placed a tentative hand on her shoulder and said, 'Sorry . . .' It was the proverbial touch that broke her back. She got up and in a very swift motion sent her hand flying to his face, getting him right in the nose. Bull's eye. He was knocked off his chair, bleeding profusely from his nostrils.

~

Before Rahul knew what hit him, two bouncers, both double his size, walked up to them.

'What is the matter here?'

'She is drunk. Everything is fine,' Rahul said and flashed his best innocent smile. He was desperately trying not to get his teeth knocked in by seven-foot giants, while clutching at his bleeding nose. The blow had broken his nose bridge.

'I am not drunk. And he is trying to . . .' she said and covered her face and started crying. At this, one bouncer grabbed him by his collar and pulled him up till only his toes were on the ground.

'Please. I am sorry. She is drunk. She is talking trash. She is a friend of mine. We are very good friends.'

'Are you two friends, ma'am?' The other bouncer asked, his arms crossed on his chest.

'No. Not at all.'

'Oh yes, we are,' Rahul pleaded weakly, a pathetic smile plastered on his battered face.

'Ask him my phone number,' Shruti said to the bouncers.

He did not have it. The bouncers looked at him to see if he had any answer.

After stuttering for a while, he spluttered, 'Umm ... I have a new phone with me ... that is why ...'

'That does not look like a new phone.' A man of authority appeared. He was more or less Rahul's age and Shruti didn't catch his face with all the lights flashing behind his head. The face became clearer and Shruti felt like she had seen the face somewhere, and then she remembered and forgot, and cried.

'I can explain,' Rahul said.

'Come with us,' the bouncers said and grabbed him by his arm and led him away.

'I can't leave her here,' he said while they were dragging him away.

'She is more safe here than with you, sir,' the guy, who seemed to be the manager, said and motioned the bouncer to take him away.

This was the last thing he heard before the bouncer punched him unconscious and dumped him outside the back door of the club.

Then they helped Shruti out of her chair and led her to the waiting lounge which accommodated single guests who had blacked out until they came back to their senses and could be transported home. She was the only one that day, and they put her on the couch and she fell asleep.

The manager sat by her side. His gaze didn't leave her face for one moment. She looked beautiful. And she was mumbling something.

23

Abhijeet and Saurav, scared out of their wits, went crazy running from door to door, asking people if they had seen Shruti, or had any idea where she would be. It took them two hours, and they had asked everybody in the building, but no one had a clue where she was. It was 2 a.m. when they, luckily, spotted Rahul's flatmate returning from his office and he told them that Rahul and Shruti were out clubbing, and they wouldn't be home until the next morning. Saurav took Rahul's number and dialled it, but it was out of reach. They told Garima about it and they decided to wait for her in her apartment.

'Why?' Garima looked at both of them and asked.

Saurav and Abhijeet were standing at two corners of the room and she was sitting on the television trolley she had bought for Shruti all those weeks ago.

They both looked at her, puzzled, waiting for her to say more.

'What?' they echoed.

'I mean this. Why this? You two are standing where you are. Shruti is God knows where with the guy she hardly knows. What did we do wrong to deserve this? Why did we have to go through this? After years, just when I thought things would be alright, it is back to where I started from. I trusted you guys with everything.

Everything. I so loved you guys, and you . . .' She broke down and covered her face. 'I was so lucky I found you. I was so lucky. You finally made my life worth living. For the first time in years, I felt good about myself. I was so happy and you guys ruined it all. You and you. Maybe me, too.' She kept sobbing.

'Everything will be okay,' Abhijeet said as he came near her.

'Nothing will be alright. Nothing will be alright! What will be alright? You were the one who drove her out. It is because of you that she isn't here. It is you. You started it with Saurav. Why? Why, Abhijeet? I was so happy and for no fault of mine, I am all alone again.'

'You have me.'

'Whatever, Abhijeet.'

'Garima,' Saurav said for the first time that evening. 'It is my fault, too. I was the one who drove Shruti away from you. And I was wrong about Riya, too. I should have waited till they had sorted things out, Riya and Abhijeet.'

'No, Saurav,' Abhijeet said. 'I was wrong with that. I should have acted more maturely. I took it a little too far. I should have given you your space. Sorry for that. But you were ignoring us for her. I mean, you should have at least talked to me about it, and I thought you would, you know.'

'I should have asked and talked to you about it. I didn't know what the deal was between the two of you.' Saurav came near and stood near Abhijeet. 'I was so fucking into her that I forgot about you guys, you, Garima . . . and even Shruti. I don't even remember the last time I talked to her. Damn, I so miss her. I am sorry, Abhijeet.'

'I am sorry, too, Saurav. I screwed it up. I am sorry for whatever I said about you and Riya,' Abhijeet mumbled.

'It is okay. I incited you to do so.'

'Still, it was me who crossed the line.'

'But I made you do so,' Saurav argued. 'What you did was understandable.'

'No, dude, it was silly.'

'What I did was silly.'

'I am sorry.'

'I am sorry too.'

They hugged. They realized it could go on and on so they stopped and hugged each other, and Garima broke out in a smile and said, 'I almost felt you guys would kiss in the end.' She rolled over laughing.

~

All three of them slumped down on the floor, onto the part which was not soiled up. Garima sat between them and put both her hands on their heads, which were on each of her shoulders and she patted them.

'I miss her. You?' she asked and Abhijeet nodded. It was still late night and they had no idea when Shruti would be back.

'Never missed anybody like this. It would have been so nice to have her here today,' Saurav said.

'It would have been so nice if the four of us were together tomorrow. Shruti and I made plans for New Year's a few weeks back. I never thought we would grow so apart when the time came. I had never wanted or looked forward to celebrating the New Year, but this time I kind of was,' Garima said.

'Damn? It's the 31st tomorrow? I had totally skipped my mind. Riya kept asking me last week about our plans, and I ignored it and now it's here? This would be my worst New Year's ever,' Saurav said.

'I have never really celebrated it anyway,' Abhijeet added, 'but this sucks.'

The three of them sat there, dejected and forlorn, and talked about Shruti and what they did to her and how unfair life had been to her, and then as the night progressed they opened up the last of Shruti's vodka and passed it around, making faces as they took long, painfully bad-tasting shots. They talked over a game of monopoly that no one concentrated on, and over the Maggi that Abhijeet cooked and it was raw, and then they drank some more.

They assured each other that everything would be okay, and Saurav would talk to his father and get Shruti a job, and then they brushed aside fears that Shruti would have to get back to her old job.

Slowly, the vodka got absorbed in their system, they got used to the pungent smell in the living room, and they ended up reasonably drunk.

'I thought a few times to hit on Shruti, especially when we went out the third time. I don't remember correctly,' Saurav reminisced.

'I remember the red dress clearly! She looked very pretty indeed,' Abhijeet remarked.

'Pretty? She looked insanely hot! You have no idea what was going on in my head,' Saurav laughed.

'I miss her,' Abhijeet said. 'It's been so long since we spent time together and just talked.' He looked at his watch and realized it was already eight in the morning. It had been six hours since they had been talking and drinking and playing and eating.

Garima then pulled his ear and said, 'Abhijeet? I miss her, too, but do you remember what *I* was wearing that day?'

'Umm, you were wearing something very nice!' he laughed and gave Saurav a high five. 'Obviously I remember, Garima. It was a short green dress, wasn't it? I remember every bit of it,' he said and pulled her cheeks.

'What?' Saurav said. 'You should have let her think that you had forgotten! Wouldn't that be fun?'

'You do that to Riya,' Garima said and everybody stopped talking. The *Riya* topic had not been raised for many hours, since the time peace was struck between these two, and before the drinking started.

'It is okay, guys,' Abhijeet said. 'I am okay with Riya. I am serious. I know you guys aren't buying it but you should. I am over that matter now.'

The other two were still silent. It is one thing to be *okay* when one is sober and knows one has people around one can hurt. It's another when one is drunk. This was the real test for truth and character.

'I will call her right now and prove it to you!' he said.

'It's early in the morning, Abhijeet. She must be sleeping,' Saurav argued.

'It's eight! For no Silverman employee, eight is early morning,' he said and called up Riya, smiling at Garima and Saurav.

24

It had been quite some time since Shruti had been sleeping in the lounge. She had talked a lot through the night, and she remembered only pieces of it. She woke up, embarrassed, and rubbed her eyes. The place was dead quiet. The lounge she was sitting in was empty and she tried to piece together events from last night. She checked her phone, but it was switched off and out of battery. She would have panicked but her head was being hammered by a million sledgehammers, and even though she tried, she couldn't think clearly.

As soon as she was about to get up, a strong male voice said from behind, 'Sit down. You had a rough night.'

She turned around to see a cup in front of her face. She took the mug and sat back down from her half-standing position. A man, rather a boy, in his mid-twenties came around and sat in front of her. His face came rushing back to her, and she remembered seeing him with two bouncers, and then she recalled the man telling her that she would be okay and she should sleep. But she felt like she had seen the face before somewhere.

'Drink. It will make you feel better.'

'Who are you?' she asked and while she sipped on the coffee, she actually *saw* him, and what a sight for sore eyes he was. His hair was wet as if he had just taken a shower, and his face clean and smooth, and it looked as if he had just slipped into a crisp blue and black striped shirt tucked into a pair of black trousers that ran across his body lines. He got to his feet, and turned, and the sight of that guy's cute butt made her burn her tongue.

She let out an *oops* and he turned back abruptly. 'Too hot?' he asked.

'Very cute. I mean, yes, it's hot. The coffee. The coffee is hot,' she said and said no further.

'I am sorry, I have to take a call. I hope you don't mind,' he said and excused himself. Even as he ambled around in the lobby, talking mostly business, Shruti felt inexplicably drawn to the man. His jawline was sharp as a knife and there wasn't an iota of fat on his body. The shirt clung to places where there were muscles, and she could clearly make out the contours of his striated chest from outside the shirt. He caught her looking at him but she couldn't tear her eyes away from his bluish grey eyes. *Have I seen him on the* Men's Health *cover? Does this guy moonlight as a model? Where have I seen him? On television?*

Even as she tried unsuccessfully to find an answer to these questions, she felt like running her hand through his hair, which was exactly what she always wanted hers to be like. Silky as hell and ridiculously glossy.

He got off the phone, and stood in front of her and waited for her to finish the coffee. She kept drinking it as if it was a glass of milk handed to her by her mother, and not the stunning Adonis standing over her. She stole a few glances at him, and suppressed an urge to cling on to his arms.

'Are you okay?' he asked and unbuttoned his sleeves and rolled them to his elbow. 'It was a long night, eh? I wasn't expecting a huge crowd a day before the 31st and we were woefully short of staff. I had to tend the bar for a couple of hours and it was terrible.'

'Hmm,' she mumbled. She thought not saying anything was a better option than saying something stupid and losing the most handsome man she had ever seen.

Looking at his rolled up sleeves, Shruti wondered if that's

how he looked after a long night, what would he look like after a shower? Or *in* the shower? She had started imagining herself being in it with him, when, all of a sudden, she realized she was *with* him, a stranger, sipping coffee in the resting room of a club, and that it was awkward and she should probably leave. The urgency of the situation crashed into her straying thoughts.

'Yes. Who are you? I am sorry I didn't ask before and I apologize if I caused trouble to you,' she said, embarrassed and nervous. 'And do you have a Nokia charger? I am out of battery. I will just charge my phone and leave.'

'I work here, and don't worry, it's all part of the job,' he said, took her phone and plugged it in the charger.

As the phone started charging, she realized she would have to go soon and she didn't want to leave the pretty guy's company. She switched on the phone and her phone started beeping with texts from Garima, and then it started ringing and it was Garima again and Shruti cut the call. Garima texted her asking when she would be back home, and Shruti texted her back telling her that she didn't know as yet, and switched off her phone.

'Your friends must be worried about you?' the guy asked.

'Yes, they were calling, but it's okay,' she answered, and fiddled with the phone, wanting to call Garima and wanting to hug her and kiss her and tell her how much she missed her.

'Where is Rahul? The guy I came here with?'

'We sent him home. He wasn't on his best behaviour last night.'

'I know. He is a bastard,' she said, recalling that it was Rahul who had gossiped about her, and not her friends. 'Did I do something stupid yesterday?'

'Not really. You just broke Rahul's nose.'

'I think I remember that. Did I say something stupid or do something stupid after that?'

'You said a lot of things. Mostly non-stupid. I can try a hand at writing your biography, but it was more of a sob story and that, too, without an ending.'

'Shit,' she said and covered her mouth.

'It's all cool. I had an interesting night. Tell me when you are ready. I will be behind that door. If you need anything, just shout out to me,' he said.

Shruti wanted to pull him down and hug him and snuggle with him and go to sleep. But she kept sitting there, looking at him, till she realized that her mouth was half open and her eyes were blank.

He smiled and walked away.

She flopped back onto the couch, grabbed a pillow and hugged it real tight, wishing it was him instead. Images came back from last night. Slowly, her face began to burn with embarrasment, because she *had* done so last night; she had hugged him and told him he was pretty and told him not to leave her alone. She saw him disappear behind the doors that had the word 'Manager' embellished on it. She was still sure she had seen him on the cover of a fitness magazine.

It took a frantic Shruti ten minutes and a bag full of cosmetics to come out all shining and fresh, as if woken up from an eight-hour sleep. She sat on the couch and held her head between her hands and thought about the sentences she had told herself last night: *I am not going back to them. It is my life. My happiness. I am not going back to Delhi. I have no friends. I have ZERO friends. They think I am a slut!*

She told herself that everything would be okay, and she wiped off the beads of tears and felt good about herself. Ten minutes passed by before she mustered the courage to finally knock on the manager's door. She took a deep breath and rapped with a confidence she did not feel.

'Come in,' he called from inside .

She entered. 'Hi.'

'Oh! You are looking . . . fresh,' he said, as he slapped down his laptop and scrutinized her.

'Thank you,' she said and looked around his office. It wasn't huge but it was tastefully done, one side of the wall was lined with books, hardbound and paperback, the other side had irregularly framed movie posters, and it all came together well.

'Where do I drop you?' he asked and got up from his chair.

'Hmmm?' The word *home* skipped her tongue, a touch of sadness came across her face and she looked down.

'Why don't we have breakfast first?' He got up and walked up to her. 'Shall we?'

'Sure,' she said, one half lost in daydreams of him, the other half thinking about the abyss that awaited her.

'Are you sure you're okay?'

'Yes, I am,' she said and they walked out of the room.

He walked down the stairs and took her hand, believing that she was still not in a good shape. She wasn't in good shape, but the reason wasn't the hangover. It was him. His hand felt like a thousand feathers on hers, only that they were strong and could have snapped her fingers into two. She walked behind him to the parking lot, unsure of the stranger, and it struck her that she hadn't yet asked his name. The beautiful stranger fetched his car keys from his back pocket, pressed the keys and the lights of a Porsche, a gleaming blue convertible, came on.

She was still standing there, waiting to make sure that it was *actually* the car she had to get into, when he opened the door and swished his hand, motioning her to sit. *As if the guy wasn't handsome enough, he had to drive a nice car too; this was just unfair. Is it really his car? Maybe not. Maybe it's his boss's car, and he is driving it around like it's his.* He backed the car out of the driveway like a maniac and drove like it was his car.

'I am sorry but I didn't catch your name,' she said.

'I am Rishab.'

'I am Shruti.'

'So, Shruti, where do you work?' he glanced at her and asked.

'Silverman Finance. I mean I used to work in Silverman Finance but I resigned,' she said, and even as she said those words, she couldn't believe them.

'Silverman Finance? I knew that you had resigned but not that it was from Silverman. I heard they are laying off a lot of people. Anyway, are you feeling any better from last night? Why are your eyes red? I hope you're not getting a fever,' he said and put the back of his palm on her forehead, and the world seemed to end, and she started to melt.

'I am okay, I think,' she said. 'Can I ask you something, Rishab?'

'Sure?' he asked.

'I feel like I have seen you somewhere. Your face is very familiar,' she said. She wanted to take his name again, which, too, sounded like a name she had heard before.

'I get that sometimes. I think I have a very common face,' he said, and she wanted to smack his gorgeous face and tell him otherwise.

'Nice car,' Shruti said, even as she wanted to say 'face' instead of 'car'.

'Thank you. It's not really mine,' he said disdainfully.

'Don't say that. You seem to be doing well. You're the manager of Elan, so that's good enough, right? Almost every second day it's in the papers, and I remember reading about the club and the man who was behind the idea. So yes, managing it is a big deal!'

'I think it's a waste of money. The same money could be better spent, and I don't consider it an achievement of any sorts,' he said.

'It's paying for your bills, Rishab,' she said. 'And you have an easy job with no boss overseeing you in the club, so that's cool, isn't it?'

'I am my own boss,' he said.

'That's an arrogant thing to say,' she responded.

'No, no, you're getting it wrong. I am my own boss. I started Elan, and it's my club,' he said, his face almost red with embarrassment.

'What? It's your club? You own it? Oh! Wait! That's how I know you! You were the one in the article. Why didn't you tell me? I have a very common face, bullshit!' she exclaimed. 'This is so cool, and strange. Why are you acting as a chauffeur to a drunken guest like me? I mean, surely, you have better things to do.'

It was his car and it was his club, and she had cut a complete fool of herself. It was *his* car? Now, she remembered the name from the article as well, and she knew he knew that she knew where he had studied, where he had grown up and what he liked and disliked. But she kept it to herself and thought better than to discuss it with Rishab.

'Tonight is the 31st night bash, so I thought I would give my people a break. And moreover, it doesn't hurt to have a beautiful girl by your side on a breakfast table, does it?' Rishab said, smiling and blushing like a child whose secret is out.

Her cheeks went red and hot, she sank into her seat, melted away and became one with the seat cushions.

'Probably, yes. Thank you,' she said, all flushed. A part of her wanted him to keep on making her feel like a million dollars, the other part wanted the beautiful, rich boy to shut up since he was so out of her league.

'Where would you like to have your breakfast, Shruti?' he asked.

'Wherever you want to. You're the fancy club owner, and so you should know all about the nice places to eat,' she mocked him and he shook his head.

'I will make it easier for you. I will drive past a few eating places. Choose the one you like.'

'Okay. Done.'

He was yet to drive by the first eating joint, when Shruti shrieked out, 'That one!' And then looked the other way as if it was a mistake.

'Which one?'

'Nothing.'

'You mean that?'

'Umm ... yes ... but it is no compulsion.' She had pointed to the small roadside dhaba that the four of them used to go to after office. They were the first ones to pass by that day. Shruti was really embarrassed to have chosen that one. Rishab drove off the road and parked the car. A boy of fourteen came to their table as soon as they settled down and said, 'Rishab *bhaiya, kya loge aaj?*'

Shruti looked at him with a shocked expression on her face.

'Not my first time. You see, every other eating joint in the city is competition. So I like this place and I was glad you chose it!'

She laughed, and acted surprised even though she remembered from the interview, and the many others she had read about him, that he liked roadside north Indian food.

25

Garima and Saurav waited for the worst while Abhijeet called Riya up, and smiled at them, and tapped his drunken feet on the floor, waiting for Riya to answer the call.

'Hi. Riya?' Abhijeet said.

'Yes. Who is this?' she asked.

'Abhijeet.'

'Hi, Abhijeet. How are you? It is so nice to hear from you. How are you?'

'Yes, Riya, how are you today? Have you seen Shruti's place? We want you to come here. Can you? Will you?'

'Yes, sure, but why?'

'We all want to see you. When is the earliest you can be here?' Abhijeet asked.

'I am not yet up, so I will see you at twelve? Give or take a few hours?' she said.

'Okay! Cool,' he said and disconnected the call. Garima and Saurav looked at each other and laughed. 'What? What?' he kept asking them for the next five minutes and they kept laughing.

It was well after an hour when Abhijeet finally got back to his senses and realized what he had done, and wondered it he had said something unwarranted.

'I knew what I was doing, people. I know I was drunk, but I also knew what I was doing.'

'Yes. I guess so. Anyway. I need to eat something,' Saurav said.

'Garima, I think it's your turn to make something now. I opened the bottles, Abhijeet made the Maggi, and now it's your turn to make paranthas or something. Garima? Garima? Lost?'

'Wait yaa, Saurav,' she said. 'I think my texts to Shruti just got delivered. Let me call her.'

She called her and Shruti disconnected the call. Garima texted her asking when she would be back home and she replied that she didn't know. Her phone was switched off again. They sat in a huddle and kept trying her phone, wondering where she was for the next hour or so and then they gave up.

'I think I need some sleep,' she said, and the others nodded, their eyes red and their bodies tired. 'Wake me up when Riya comes over.'

The three of them found couches, and bedspreads, and slept wherever they found space. It was not until two in the afternoon that they got up, slightly hungover and hungry.

Garima made coffee for the three of them, and they missed their toothbrushes and a good night's sleep. They had forgetton they had called Riya over, and Riya who had lost Shruti's address had called them multiple times and no one had picked up her calls. Saurav called her up and explained to her the route to Shruti's place, and then laughed at Abhijeet for the drunken call he had made.

They all talked in incomprehensible mumbles, groaning and cursing about why they drank so much the night before. It wasn't until another hour that they felt sane and normal.

'Hey, guys,' Garima said. 'I have an idea. Let's decorate this place! What say? A sorry, plus a New Year's party? And then we will call everyone over and have a big bash?'

'Everyone?' Abhijeet asked.

'I mean Deb and Avantika. Sameer?'

'Then we will need food, won't we?' Saurav asked.

'Fine by me,' Abhijeet said.

'But then, when do we order the food and stuff?' Saurav asked. 'I am dying of hunger, man. Any longer and I would eat you guys up!'

'We'll need five pizzas? Or do you want six?' Garima said.

'Okay then, ten pizzas on the way,' he said, flicked up his car keys and barged through the door before anybody could say anything, leaving Garima and Abhijeet smiling at each other.

'I need to brush,' Abhijeet said.

'Call Saurav and ask him to get the necessities,' she said and Abhijeet called Saurav and asked him to get three toothbrushes and toothpaste.

'We need to get the house in order,' Garima said, with both her hands on her waist. She let out a deep sigh and stared at Abhijeet.

'Don't tell me you want me to get all this cleaned up,' he said and looked the other way.

'As a matter of fact, I do.'

'*Arey*, we will do it *together*. What will *you* do if I do this?' he protested.

'We need to decorate this place. I will go and get balloons, and frills, and other stuff. I will go get those.'

'Please let me go. You will have to walk so far to get them. Or let me come with you and then we will do it together,' he argued.

'And why should I do it? It's not my responsibility!'

'We are in this mess with Shruti because of you and Saurav! So I'm certainly not cleaning *this* mess in her apartment! Now shut up and get to work, and by the time I come back, this should be clean,' she said and left before he could protest more.

He looked at the floor and then looked heavenwards.

26

They had ordered more than their fill that day. Hot *laccha* paranthas with dollops of butter, and bowls of thick daal, and then they finished off with a glass each of frothing lassi.

'Now that's real food,' Rishab said and hardly kept from burping. The plates were licked clean in a matter of minutes, and even though they were full to their noses, they wanted to eat more. '*Ab bas*, I need my bed and a warm quilt to doze off! Brilliant start to a great day.'

'True,' she said with a bit of sadness in her voice, which Rishab was quick to catch.

'Unless, of course ... Ms Shruti,' he leant forward, 'has some other plans?'

'Other plans? No,' she said. 'You have had a long day, you really need to sleep. Thank you for this. But I can't take more of your time, and moreover you have a long night today to take care of, don't you?'

'You are not taking my time. I am wilfully offering it to you! Shall we?' He thrust out his hand to pull her out of her chair.

'Rishab, I think I need to go now,' she said. 'I really have to go.'

'Why? Is there somebody waiting?'

'No, but ...'

'Then shut up and tell me if you want to catch a movie? Just name the first movie that comes to your mind!'

'I don't know, *New York*?'

'Okay, *New York*!' he said. 'Will you drive?'

'I can't drive! Not this.'

'Have a licence?'

'Yes, I do, but I have never really driven. I just use it as a proof of my age.'

'Here.' He threw the keys to her.

She looked at the keys and the four buttons on it, all of which seemed equally capable of opening the car. She pressed one and nothing happened. She pressed all and the car opened, started to beep and light up, and Rishab pressed three of them and it stopped and they got in.

'These things are a little funny,' he chuckled.

'Shut up. Whatever happened to insert and open?' she asked, exasperated and always nervous.

'That can have many connotations, actually?'

'Dirty mind,' she said and rolled her eyes.

'Thank you.'

'Whatever.'

She turned the key, and turned it way too far and the car grumbled. Rishab cringed but still managed a smile.

'I am sorry,' she grinned ruefully. 'I told you I can't drive this.'

'You can drive it, it's no big deal.'

'Oh yes, why not! I am used to driving gleaming new Porsches with someone like you sitting next to me,' she mocked.

'Excuse me?'

'Nothing. Just shut up,' she said. Rishab smiled. 'And anyway, if I bang this thing into anything, you know I can't afford even a headlight. So it'll be your loss.'

'It's not really my loss, it would be ideally my dad's loss, and I really don't care,' he said, and Shruti rolled her eyes, pushed the accelerator and tried to negotiate the car out of the parking and it was a horrendous attempt. But after putting Rishab through many moments when he wanted to shout and cringe and jump out of the car and lay prostate in front of it so that she could run him over instead, she did better, changing gears on time and driving smoothly. A feather touch and the car was already doing eighty.

'Take a left from there,' he pointed.

'Rishab, you want to watch it for sure?' she asked.

'You chose the movie. Why? You don't want to see it?'

'No. I mean, I can drive this for three hours. You go and watch the movie,' she laughed.

'You seriously want to drive this for three hours? For one, I absolutely hate driving!'

'I mean, I can. It is probably the first time, and the last, I am going to sit in a car like this. And obviously, you hate driving! You're a rich spoilt kid, owner of club and fancy cars and toys. This must be like something you're bored of,' she mocked and laughed.

'Don't patronize me! And I would love it if you can keep driving. I always dreamed of a date, where my girl would drive!'

'Your girl?' she said with scorn. It is another matter that her brain erased everything else to accommodate the memory of these two words and several copies of them, and then made copies of the copies.

'Umm . . . I mean, the girl with me.' For the first time, he fumbled with words, and he blushed.

'Date?'

'Yes, that is true. It is a date, isn't it?' he asked.

'Okay, I will give that one to you. One question though?'

'Shoot,' he said and pointed to a direction that led to a highway. She was cruising between ninety kilometres to a hundred kilometres an hour now.

'How many *my girls* have there been like me? The ones you talk sweetly to and sweep off their feet with your charming smile, your big car, and by dropping in casually, mid-conversation, that you own the biggest club in India.'

'You wouldn't want to know,' he smirked.

'Okay.' She clenched the steering wheel in anger.

'But you are the first one to drive my car!'

'Thanks for the privilege,' she said wryly.

'You are welcome. But tell me? Are you jealous? Why does it look like you are jealous? You're jealous, right?'

'Why would I be? Why would I care if this is what you do with a zillion other girls? I am sure you have a lot of girls around you. Why should I care?'

'Maybe because you have started liking me?' he suggested gently, his eyes twinkling with boyish mischief.

She wanted to thrust her head out from the sun roof and shout out to the world that she was on a date with most gorgeous boy ever, but she said, 'I don't like you a bit.'

'Then why are you with me right now?' he smiled again.

'First, I am jobless. Second, I have nothing to do. And third, I am hoping to use you to get myself a job somewhere! Maybe I can be a bartender or something.'

'How mean, Shruti.'

'That is how I am,' she said and shrugged her shoulders. 'I am just using you.'

'I like you the way you are.'

'Are you flirting with me?'

'Actually that depends on whether it's working. Is it?' he asked.

'No, it's not, Rishab.'

'Then, I am not flirting with you at ALL,' he said and shook his head from side to side.

'You know what, I have heard these dialogues from somewhere,' she said. 'Oh yes, it's from *Get Smart*. You have seen the movie, right?'

'I watch every movie that is released, be it from Bollywood or Hollywood. In fact, I even watch a lot of south Indian movies. Aren't they hilarious?'

'Why did you miss *New York* then? We could have watched the movie,' she said.

'I already saw the movie a few days back when John Abraham and the director of the movie held a special screening for a few of their friends, and I was invited,' he said, looked at her and smiled.

'You're such a show off,' she said and drove on. He laughed.

27

It was tougher than he had anticipated. Abhijeet had gloves on, taken from Shruti's haircolour box, and two handkerchiefs tied around his mouth and nose. He wished he could have one on his eyes too.

He nearly puked twice while scraping off the dried portions of the vomit, and he started hating Shruti and alcohol with every passing moment. Just as he was done pouring water over the floor for the umpteenth time that morning, there was a knock on the door.

He opened the door, thinking it would be Garima and he could thrust his smelly hands out and shout from beneath his handkerchiefs, 'Smell this!' Riya dodged his outstretched hands and that's when he saw it was not Garima.

'Hi,' he said.

'What?' she asked.

'Hi, Riya,' he said again, before he realized that his voice was getting muffled beneath the handkerchiefs on his mouth and he took them off.

'Hi, Abhijeet.'

'Hi. Long time. Sit, sit. I am sorry for the mess. Actually it isn't mine. I am just cleaning it up because Saurav and Garima are out and I have to do it.'

'Do you need help?'

'I can sure do with some,' he said and she gave him the same beamer that she used to give him during their college days.

'You look cool with those handkerchiefs on your face. Can I get one too? The colour suits your eyes, and hey, I had that handkerchief, too, the Winnie the Pooh one, really cute and guess what, they were on sale! Cool, huh?'

'That is indeed nice. There.' He passed one to her.

She put on the handkerchief and said, 'Now we are ready.' She took a wiper in hand. 'Let's do some cleaning!' she smiled, showing all thirty-two of her teeth. Her enthusiasm regarding the littlest of things was exactly as it was when he knew her.

Together, they took well over half an hour to make that place shine as it had never before. Then they dusted every surface to a gleam!

'Here. Come, let's take a picture,' Riya declared, once they were done. She put her cell phone on self-timer and placed it on the television. They both stood side by side with handkerchiefs on their heads and mouths and wipers in hand. 'Not like this. No!' Riya shouted, as soon as the first picture got clicked.

She set the camera on the self-timer again and positioned Abhijeet and herself in a pose she thought would look good. Then came a million different poses and a zillion more pictures.

They were exhausted from running to and fro from the camera and posing in the mere ten seconds that they had. Riya was never satisfied with one take. She took five of each at least, much to Abhijeet's frustration. They sat down on the bed that they had now rolled out and spread a nice blue bed sheet on.

They exchanged nothing for the next two minutes, just caught hold of their breath and smiled at whatever had just happened in last one hour. The other two had not yet returned.

'Riya. I am sorry. I know I said a lot of things I shouldn't have. I am really really sorry about that,' he said.

'So, finally,' she said and rubbed her palms together. Then, she smiled wickedly, 'The stubborn creature realizes his mistake!'

'That is rude.'

'Yes, I know. I am sorry. I should have understood you back then. But seriously, I really liked you and loved you as a friend. You were the only perfect part of my life back then. And once you went, everything fell apart. The movies, the dance, everything became history. I turned into you. Books, professors, assignments and I don't know why but I so wanted you to be around during those days. But . . .' She now had tears in her eyes. 'And yes, you were right. He left me, no prizes for guessing that,' she said and smiled a little.

'Good for you.'

'And see, I am almost where you are! You should be proud of yourself. It is probably because of you that I am here, at Silverman Finance,' she said. Her tone alternated between a sad and a sprightly one.

Her eyes had started to get wet when Abhijeet got up and took her in his arms and then she started crying a little more, before crying a lot more. They stood there for quite some time, before she broke out of his embrace and looked at him with her cutest smile and tears in her eyes and said, 'You were my best friend, you are my best friend, and you will always be! Whether you like it or not.' She broke out of his hug completely and said, 'I will show you something.'

'What it is?' he asked.

'Just wait,' she said and started looking around for her handbag. She rummaged through it, took something out and walked up to Abhijeet. 'Something I had kept for posterity, for this day and the days that we will celebrate our friendship,' she said and kept three stapled clutches of pages on the table and said, 'Assignments . . . that is law . . . and . . .' she said.

'. . . macro,' he said.

'And economics.'

They hugged. They looked each other in the eye and Abhijeet said, 'Missed you.'

'Missed you, too.'

'I love you so much.'

'I love you, too,' she said and they came close and they were almost about to kiss, their lips briefly touching, before they realized that they shouldn't and they parted.

'I am sorry. I didn't mean to do that,' he said.

'I am sorry, too, though I wouldn't mind kissing you some day,' she said and smiled playfully.

'Neither would I,' he said.

They both laughed and hugged, and they both knew they had wanted to kiss each other once, just to see how it felt like.

28

'You know John Abraham? You do? Or you just knew the director of the movie? You don't know him, do you?'

'Yes. Why? You like him?'

'Umm, not really, I am more a Shahrukh Khan fan. But I think you are too rich to understand that meeting superstars is a big thing for people like us. I have friends who show off their pictures with Shahrukh and Aamir when they were three years old,' she mocked.

'Okay, okay!'

'Whatever,' she said.

'See that is why I hate being who I am.'

'Now what did I say that made you say that?' she asked.

'I say things or do things that are very natural and everyday to me and people think I am arrogant. I have not lived your kind of life. They think I don't know what hardship is in life and discredit me for everything I do. Maybe I have got everything in life but there is also a possibility that I might have earned it, too.'

'Elaborate.'

'I could be as good as you are. If I were in your place, I might have got where you are. Getting into Silverman Finance is a big deal and I know that. But I might have been that good and maybe I am. But just because I have every comfort in the world and was born with a silver spoon in my mouth, that doesn't give the people the right to wrest away credit for everything I do. They will have just one thing to say. *Dad's money making the way for the son.* And believe me, hearing that is way worse than not getting clicked with superstars,' he said and looked away.

'Yes. That is true. But I wonder sometimes why you people never go to Indian colleges. You still choose the easy path. I have a friend who is quite rich . . . may not be as rich as you are, but he is an IITian. Why not you?'

'Saurav?'

'Yes,' she said.

She was impressed that he remembered it from her previous night's blabbering.

'See, Shruti. When you have pots of Dad's money lying around, you wouldn't like to be a speck in the engineering world. And when you see that kind of money, the only thing that gets drilled into your mind by your family is to concetrate on how to make more out of it. This guy you are talking about, what do his parents do?'

'Engineer and doctor.'

'See my point? It is how you are bred,' he continued with authority dripping from his voice. 'When I was young, I dropped out of business school for this project and I have been toiling hard. Yes, I don't have to catch buses and autos, but I am working. And hard enough. I know this nightclub thing might seem like too frivolous a venture to start your business with. Something like, oh, it's like a rich man's wife doing an interior designers' course. But let me tell you, it is not easy. My point is—I am rich and that is not my fault. It has been two years and this place will break even in four and that counts as a success. For me, at least. People may attribute it to my dad, but I will fiercely defend it as mine,' he said and looked ahead.

'Point taken,' she said, and wondered how old he might be. That is one part of the interview she couldn't remember: *how old was the heir to the group of Manchanda Industries?* She wondered why

Rishab had not yet mentioned his father's huge business empire and that he was the successor to the second richest man in India. She didn't want to mention it either. Ignorance is bliss, and she wouldn't do anything to jeopardize the best date ever.

They drove on the highway for a little while, after which she got a little bored and asked, 'What next? I am getting a little bored. I can see why you hate driving. It does get a little monotonous after a bit.'

'Oh, are you bored? Do you want to feel a rush?'

'Umm ... yes ...' she said sceptically. 'What do you have in mind?'

'Have you raced an aircraft?' he asked and a boyish smile came back on his face.

'What? Do I look like I might have done it? What makes you think I might have done it?'

'The question is whether *you* want to do it?'

'Are you drunk? Are you kidding me? Are you nuts?'

'No, no, and yes!' he said gleefully and she was already sold.

'Okay. You do it as I am none of the above. I will watch.'

'You're coming with me,' he said.

'Are you serious?' she asked now. She had thought he was kidding.

'Hell, yeah,' he said like a little boy.

They stopped, switched seats and drove onto the highway. He nodded at a person who was at what looked like a runway. The guy let them through the guarded barricade. They stopped there for a while.

'Look,' he pointed to a small jet approaching the runway in his rearview mirror.

'Oh shit. You are really gonna race that?' she asked and clasped her palms to her face.

'Seems like . . . Yes!'

'Don't do it.'

'Why?'

'I am a little scared.'

'Good.' He pushed on the gas and the car was surrounded by white smoke and burnt rubber.

The jet was a kilometre away, and then it shattered the glass of the shiny blue Porsche as it passed them by, and made the car seem like a small toy. Rishab clenched the wheel and let the brakes go.

First second. 20 km/hr.

Second. 69 km/hr.

Third. 92 km/hr.

They both hit the back of their seats. Any faster and they would have broken their necks. The car was hurtling to the infinite now. The road was getting blurred. The car had started shaking and wobbling and they could smell burnt rubber. They were surrounded by car smoke.

Fourth second. 145 km/hr.

The car was zooming now. A few more seconds and the beast reached 185 km when they left the jet behind, and the car wobbled like crazy. Undeterred, Rishab pushed on the gas further.

He was going at 210.

One rock and the car would have smashed to pieces.

'Stop it! Oh shit!' Shruti wanted to shout out but her voice failed. She closed her eyes and grabbed onto the sides of the seat. Her stomach was churning and she felt like she would puke, and had it been anyone other than Rishab, she would have.

The car had started to vibrate wildly, seeming it would topple over. They had both been pushed back to the seat and they could feel the air fighting them. The sights had gone. They could see just two colours—blue of the sky and a blurred brown road ahead.

The jet was slowing down and was about to land. He gave the car its last thrust and pushed on the pedal. It touched 250 km/hr and the jet touched down. They were flying. She felt weightless.

He won!

Rishab waved at the pilot and the pilot gave him a thumbs-up.

They just came to a stop and he took the last bit out of the tyres by doing a 360-degree turn a few yards in front of the jet. Shruti's head spun.

'It is over,' he whispered in her ear. She opened her eyes, still in a daze. She rushed out of the car and slammed the door. She bent down with her palms against the knees, panting.

Rishab came out and said, 'I am sorry, but I couldn't have stopped midway. And by the way, I won.' He thought she would puke, too. There had been guys who had puked.

'Are you okay?' he asked and bent down.

She looked at him, still bent, 'Can we do it again?'

'But you closed your eyes.'

'Obviously, I closed my eyes! This was my first time! But now I regret it. It was so good,' she said and held him by his arm.

'I know.'

They kept standing there looking back at the runway and the barren lands they had whizzed past. It was quite a distance and took just a few seconds.

'I think I now have to thank you for a lot of things,' she said. 'I will treat you some day if you allow me to.'

'Treat me today,' he said, almost in a reflex.

'Today? I think you should rest. We should really be going home now. It is the 31st today and a big day for your club. We should be going now.'

'Oh! Big businesswoman, you are! Shut up and stop telling me what I have to do! I am sure I will manage everything right.'

'So, where are we going?' she asked, embarrassed. 'This time you can choose and I will drive and you point out where you want to eat.'

'I have kind of decided. It is Palates of the World. I really like that restaurant and it's been days that I have eaten there and I would like it if we can go there,' he said.

'Perfect. Palates of the World it is. Can I drive?'

'Yes. You can. But there is a slight problem.'

'What?'

'I don't think you have a licence to get us there,' he said, dejected.

'Oh, yes I do!'

'No, you don't, Shruti. The restaurant is in Delhi.'

'What?'

'And we are flying,' he said, turned her around and pointed to the jet standing there.

She fainted.

29

'Did we interrupt?' Saurav came in balancing a few pizza boxes and a few bottles of coke. Abhijeet was hugging Riya when he came in. Along with him came Garima and both of them smiled seeing them together. A few minutes earlier and they would have caught Abhijeet and Riya almost kissing!

All of them hugged in pairs, all the six possibilities in varying degrees of tears in their eyes.

'I have heard a lot about you,' Garima said to Riya.

'I hope it was more good than bad,' Riya chuckled. 'And you have the most beautiful eyes ever EVER EVER. And I just love those earrings you wore that day! Where did you get them from? By the way, we cleaned up the house if you haven't noticed!'

Garima and Saurav looked around and they were suitably impressed. They sat down, opened two pizza boxes, a bottle of Coke, and started talking.

Riya and Abhijeet narrated their story to Saurav and Garima, and Garima told Riya about Shruti and how they had messed up her life. That reminded Garima to call Shruti again, whose phone was now switched on, but the call was disconnected. 'Text her,' Saurav said and she did, and Shruti replied that she wouldn't be back home before night or later. A little later, her phone was out of reach.

It was already evening when the four of them started working on the balloons and the charts, one of which said 'Happy New Year' and the other said 'We Are Sorry'. The charts were half the size of each wall and were in blazing red on a white background and they emptied tubes after tubes of sparkles all over the chart. Satisfied with what they had done, they hauled up the charts onto the walls and nailed them in. They went on to plaster the other walls with frills, Christmas balls and stars, till the whole room was a glittering mess, and they knew they had gone a little overboard with everything. The worst part was blowing the balloons though, and without a pump, it took the four of them two hours to blow up every balloon—their jaws hurt once they finished.

Saurav ordered two four-pound cakes and two more pizzas, two crates of beer, three vodka bottles and ten bottles of Sprite for the party they were not sure they would have. They warmed up the left-over pizzas from the morning, downed them with a few bottles of Coke and felt tired and sleepy.

It was ten at night when the four of them finally woke up, ten minutes after the incessant ringing of the bell by the delivery guys. They took the delivery of the cakes and sat in a circle. They rubbed their eyes and yawned, none of them in any mood to party that night; if anything, they wanted to go to sleep again. Shruti was still untraceable; Garima called on her number incessantly and each of her calls were disconnected.

'I have no idea what she is upto! Is he still with Rahul?' Garima asked. 'Will you please check next door with Rahul's roommate?'

Saurav nodded and went next door to check with Rahul's roommate, but the flat was locked.

'What if something happened to her?' Garima asked, fearing the worst. 'I should text her.'

'Let us know if you're fine,' she texted Shruti, and the reply came, *'I'm fine. The three of you don't need to worry about me. I am doing great without you. Shruti.'* Garima instantly broke down in tears. Seeing that, Abhijeet, angry and disappointed, started calling Shruti from his number, and the phone rang incessantly at first and then went out of reach.

The house was still decorated as such, only that the posters had moved down from one of the corners and nobody was interested enough to set them right. They had slept well and they wanted to sleep more.

Saurav pulled out another mattress from the bedroom and a couple of quilts, turned up the air-conditioner and the four of them tucked themselves inside the quilts. It was lovely feeling, as the couples hugged and lay there exchanging sweet nothings and telling each other how lucky they were to have each other in their lives. They had now realized how futile it was to have a great party, and that all successful New Year's plans are the ones that are spent watching Bollywood stars dancing and receiving awards, tucked in quilts with the people you care about.

At the back of their minds, they were thinking of Shruti, who was somewhere out there with somebody they didn't know. They were terribly worried about her. More than that, they were slightly jealous because she was doing fine and she didn't need them to be near for even the New Year. They wanted her back. They wanted things to be as they were. They wanted their group to be complete again.

30

Rishab helped Shruti onto the stairs of the jet, where a man in a butler's uniform and two men in pilot's uniforms were waiting to greet them.

'Good morning, Shruti,' the pilots echoed.

'Good morning ma'am,' the butler said, as he handed out towels to both of them. Rishab led her to the main sitting area, and told her that he could impress her by flying the aircraft himself but then he wouldn't be able to concentrate on her, and she blushed on hearing that.

'How do they know my name?'

'Technology has come a long way, sweetheart,' he whispered. 'I mean I texted them.' He chuckled.

They sat down in two huge, black Lazy Boy type chairs and the butler/waiter served them water, after which Rishab asked him to leave them alone for a while.

'One question, Rishab. Just one question.'

'Shoot.'

'Just exactly how much money does your dad have?' she said and stared and waited to see if Rishab would tell her what she already knew. *What is there to hide?* she asked herself.

He laughed. 'We have three of these.'

'You must be having it tough making your ends meet, Rishab. Only three of these?'

'Yes,' he chuckled.

She sat back up in her seat and asked, 'Are you mentally retarded?'

'Why? Why are you saying that?'

'No, seriously. Where is that butler, I should ask him,' she said. 'I mean why all this? I mean why *me*? Why not some starlet? Model? Anyone? Why me? This doesn't make any sense. I have never seen the inside of a Porsche. Or a jet. And I have never seen you before. Anyone who would look at this from the outside would think of me as a gold-digger, or a girl who is trying to ensnare a rich guy because he is insanely wealthy and his father owns nightclubs and cars and jets!'

'If I had a reason, I would give it to you, but I don't. I would try to string together words and try to charm you unsuccessfully, but in the simplest of words I think I couldn't let you go.'

'Not convincing enough,' she kicked back and drifted away. It was hard for her to believe that she wasn't just another girl Rishab wanted to lay. She would have fallen for his words had he been just Rishab, the son a rich father, but Rishab's surname added a lot many layers to who he was. She tried hard not to think too much into the unrealness of what was happening and, slowly, drifted off.

A loud rumbling of the plane shook her and she got up. She was tightly strapped and safe . . . and she noticed, tucked in neatly by Rishab in a nice warm blanket.

'Delhi.'

'Are you for real or should I go back to sleep?' she asked groggily with a smile. 'Because none of this feels real.'

'It's very real.' He got up and pecked her on her cheek. 'Let's go.'

Shruti sat there with a hand on her cheek and eyes wide open, too shocked to believe what had just happened. Not just what happened a second ago, but what was happening since morning. The day before, she had lain sloshed in her apartment with no one to call her own and now she was in Delhi, with this mysteriously good-looking and awesomely rich guy, sitting in his jet on New Year's Eve.

'Let's go,' he now said in a firmer tone.

'Yes, sure. Let us go. No problem,' she mocked. 'I was in Hyderabad this morning and I am in Delhi now. No problem whatsoever . . .' her voice trailed off as she got up.

There was a car waiting for them at the footsteps of the step ladder of the aircraft, it was an Mercedes convertible, and they drove for about an hour, after which they reached Greater Kailash, where he had picked out the restaurant. The doorkeeper of the restaurant knew her name, too, and she gave the same bewildered look to him. They went inside and the place she thought would be brimming with people was empty.

Instead, a huge banner had the words, *WELCOME SHRUTI*, written on it, hung right in front of them. She looked at him and he looked back and smiled. Shocks had become the order of the day and now they failed to register. They sat down at a corner table and the pianist started belting out some really great-sounding tunes.

'I miss them,' she said. A tear rolled off her pretty face and wet the napkin below.

'Everything is going to be all right. We will talk to them once we are in Hyderabad,' he assured her.

'*We*?'

'I mean, if you want me to, I can talk to them.' He came to sit next to her. He took her hands into his and looked at her.

'Are we meeting again?' she looked at him teary-eyed.

'Had my mother been alive I would have had her meet you. You're that sweet. Does that feel like we are meeting again?'

'No, I just thought . . . I am sorry. I don't know. You are good-looking . . .'

'Am I?' he asked and smiled.

'You know you are . . . you have all this . . .' She pointed to the restaurant.

'This is not mine, it's rented.'

'Not my point! You are rich, good-looking, smart and everything. And most importantly, you don't know me. Why are you doing this, Rishab?'

'Do you think that after last night, I don't know you?'

'Did I sleep with you?'

'NO! You didn't! But you talked a lot and I feel I know you for years. I have never heard someone talk for that long.'

'Please don't show me dreams that would eventually . . .'

'This is not a dream.'

They sat there, hand in hand, till it was late evening. They boarded the flight back to Hyderabad just before 10.00 p.m. Just as she boarded the plane, Garima started calling her again and she kept disconnecting the calls. Garima texted her asking if she were okay and she texted back saying that she was doing great without them. Within seconds Abhijeet started calling her and it took all her strength not to receive the call and tell him how much she missed every one of them.

Shruti had pestered him to go back to Hyderabad before it struck 12 and be there at his nightclub that night. All her fervent requests were turned down and she was categorically told to shut up till the time they reached the club.

They reached Hyderabad just in time and rushed to the club. Rishab drove like a maniac as he had sworn to her that he wouldn't say a thing before they reached the club and it was getting mighty difficult for him to do so. Rishab pecked her once or twice when they stopped at red lights, and she made a purring sound every time and went back to sleep.

'I had a great time today,' Rishab said, as they stood outside the back entrance of Elan. The parking lot of Elan was choc-a-bloc with cars. 'You know what?' Rishab said, starting to walk away. 'I don't care about the party any more. And since you care so much about the party tonight, I think you should go and attend it.'

'*What?* I don't own this place, you do, Rishab! Are you out of your mind? Just go inside and have your moment,' she protested.

'No. Come with me, I will show you something,' he said and started rushing towards the road and waited for Shruti to catch up.

'What the . . .'

He crossed the road and reached the other side where there was a half-built apartment where construction seemed to have been stopped long back and waited for her. She ran and joined him, cursing Rishab for his stupidity.

'Where are we going?' Shruti asked, as Rishab led her into darkness. 'I think you should go back to Elan.'

They crossed the half-broken, rusted brown gate of the apartment. There were mounds of hardened cement and sand everywhere and stray dogs had made this place their haven. It was pitch-dark. There were truck trails everywhere with a broken-down truck lying upside down at a distance. It looked like it had been years since anyone had been there. There were no traces of human existence and barring the croaking of crickets, there was an eerie silence all around them.

'Just come.' He clutched her hand again and they jumped on the mounds and entered what would have been the lobby of the building. They reached the bottom of the flight of stairs which went up twenty-three storeys and they could see the moonlight coming in through the terrace of the building.

'Where?' she asked.

'Up there,' he pointed upwards.

Before she could say anything, he had already started going up the stairs and was pulling her up with him. They went on climbing the stairs, Rishab out of instinct and Shruti following him step for step.

They had climbed five storeys now and the darkness engulfed them. Shruti had started panting and was running out of breath.

Without asking for permission, he turned around and pulled her to him. In one fluid motion, he swept her feet off the ground and picked her up. She was off the ground now, with one arm around his neck and one looped from the front, clutching the first one. She wanted to scream out as she looked down the stairs which had no railing, but she felt safe in his arms; he strode up the stairs, as if she weighed nothing. She kept her head close to his chest. She felt like losing herself in him. She already had.

'I can walk,' she murmured half-heartedly.

'I know,' he said and kept walking up the stairs. His grasp was strong and his legs did not miss a pace.

Shruti thought, if she was ever to fall in love again, it would be now. Rishab was everything she ever wanted, he was everything everyone promised her.

Rishab's stride never slackened, as he walked up floor after floor. They got nearer to the light. Shruti looked down once and her stomach churned. They reached the twenty-third floor of what was planned to be the terrace of that building and set her down. He walked to the edge of the roof and said, 'See,' and pointed in the direction of the club.

She saw Elan beautifully illuminated with all kinds of lights. She could not hear a thing but she could feel the beat of the music thump against the windows of the club. She looked around to see the entire city of Hyderabad lit up. It was full of activity; there were cars buzzing around, buses, autos, all looking like specks from up there. They were far removed from the chaos, the rush and the revelry.

He went further to the edge of the building and sat with his legs dangling down from there. Shruti was looking at him from a distance, too scared to say anything.

'Rishab, come back from there,' she said. The terrace had no railing and it scared the shit out of her.

He didn't reply. He looked back and motioned her to come near. With trembling feet and hands, she gave her hand to him and sat down beside him. She looked down almost thirty storeys. Her heart pounded as Rishab pulled her close and clutched on to him with all her life. They were sitting with nothing under their feet but a dark thirty-storey drop. She looked down, her stomach felt strange and she hung on to him harder.

'This is my favourite place, ever since I was twelve.' He looked at her and held her hand in his, started to caress them slowly. He continued, 'This was to be built in my mother's name. It was my mother's dream. She wanted this to be an office that would be the nerve centre of all the schools and colleges she wanted to open for the poor. She wanted her office to be right here, where we are sitting. My father thought it was a waste of money. Mom had never asked for anything in life except this. He could well afford it. But he couldn't see his money not making more money. He thought my mother wanted this because she had nothing to do. Once she died, this never got completed ... He never got time from sleeping with female starlets who were younger than I was.' He stopped and a few tears hit her hands. He collected himself, started staring at a distance and continued, 'He wanted to convert this into an upscale residential apartment. The government didn't allow that and he stopped the investment. He blocked all funds. I talked to him and he said business can't be compromised for dead people's dreams,' Rishabh rasped and paused.

'He tried to sell it off but nobody would take it. I was still studying when I overheard my dad talking to somebody who was ready to buy it. I left everything and came here. I came here and asked my father for the funds to open Elan. That loud, terrible place needed more money than this, and we had to bribe the whole state for it. But my father didn't mind. I told him this place, this unfinished office building, would be a huge hotel facing Elan some day. He didn't sell it because he believed it could be done. But it will not be a hotel, it will be the way Mom wanted it. This is what my dream is,' he said. 'Not that.' He pointed to the club.

He wasn't crying any more. They were quiet for a while. Shruti didn't say a word. She didn't have anything to say.

'I have never talked to anyone about it and I don't know why I told you this. But when you talked to me last night, I thought we had something in common. We don't have a family we can go back to, we don't have a father we could rely on and I know it's strange but I thought I could finally tell someone about the angst I felt all these years. I didn't want to let you go. And trust me, you are not the first beautiful, drunk girl that I have met but you're the only one I wanted to spend time with.'

'Okay,' she said with a frown.

'I mean, yes ... As in, you are the most beautiful of all of them ... and the most charming one, too ... When I saw you last night, I don't know, I couldn't move an inch. I sat there the entire night, just looking at you as you spoke, cried, balled up and slept so peacefully. I envied you. I wanted that calm. I know all this is not making sense at all, but I totally got hooked. I wished the night would last forever. I don't know what love is, I don't want to know what it is, and I don't know whether it is this. All I know is that I wished you wouldn't blow me off this morning. All I wished was that I could talk to you once. All I wanted was for you to stay with me. Deep inside, I wished it would go as it is going right now.' He put his hand out and she put hers into his. He pulled her near and hugged her.

He slipped his hand into his pocket and put on a slow English number that Shruti didn't recognize, but it was good enough to slow dance to, especially with her head against his shoulder.

'Shruti, that is a dream that fades. You are a dream that I hope never will. I never wish to wake up, if it is one. I don't know what this is, but whatever it is, I sure like it. I sure like you. And I sure like *us*. The first smile you gave this morning, it is still here. I remember those lips curving to give your face that glow that is still lighting up my life. I know it sounds crazy, but if I have ever felt . . . ever, *ever* felt that there is something to really live for and live by for the rest of this life, it is today. I don't know where we go from here, I don't know what will happen from here, but whatever happens, this day will be my most cherished one. You will be my most cherished person.'

'But . . . why me?' she asked, as she looked up from her embrace, still teary-eyed.

'I don't have an answer.'

He looked at her staring at him, clutched her tighter and moved his head close to her.

'What I do know is that this has been my best New Year ever.' He bent over and she closed her eyes. She waited to be kissed.

He looked at her face, gleaming under the moonlight. The wind made her hair fall on her face; he stroked her hair and tucked a lock behind her ear, not letting her move. He closed his eyes and moved his head closer to hers. She could feel his breath and her pulse racing. He bent down to her face, his lips touched hers.

Fireworks went off, coming through the unfinished roof off the Elan, filling up the sky in blue and red lights, while they kissed. Her lips firmly enveloped in his and his in hers, their tongues twirled each other's around, while the embrace got stronger. Shruti hung on to him with curled toes, as Rishab slipped her shirt off her shoulder and kissed her. Her hands started working on his shirt, unbuttoning it. She lost her footing and Rishab grabbed her to bring her back from the edge.

His hands slipped in and moved up her back. She clawed, as she cringed and bit his shoulder.

She climbed onto him as his hands gripped her and slipped the shirt off her.

'Rishab . . . Take this off . . .' She pulled at his vest.

'Not fair.' He tugged at her bra.

'Don't even think about it,' she threatened.

'Try me.' He put her on the ground, gripped her close and turned her around and rendered her naked.

'Oh . . .' she said as she turned around and hugged him, her breasts crushing against his chest, her nails clawing on his back. 'It's not fair,' she said and he smirked. Within fraction of a second, she could feel his bare body against hers, the contours of his muscles rammed and pounded and glided against her body, and she felt she would pass out in ecstasy. His fingers on her skin felt like a million stars had burst inside her and she wanted it to never end. They fought. They bit. They clawed.

Fireworks lit up the sky.

31

New Year's Eve came and went and the four of them kept lying there. The vodka had already been opened and so had the beers while they watched Indian movie and television stars dance and bring in the New Year. Since they had realized nobody was coming home, they took it on themselves to see to it that not a drop of it was wasted. They were totally sloshed by the time the clock turned 12 and were taking turns at the washroom, puking and cursing the alcohol.

Soon afterwards, they all lay down and dozed off. It was three in the night when Saurav's phone rang in Shruti's bedroom.

'What?' Riya got up and asked sleepily.

'I will get it.' Saurav kissed her and got up to get the phone. He hoped it was Shruti, but it wasn't her.

'Yes, who is this?' Saurav croaked.

'Rajat Thapar.'

'Yes, sir! Happy New Year. How can—'

'Cut the crap, Saurav. What do you think you will do?' Thapar was frantic. He was calm by other people's standards, but frantic by his.

'I don't get it.'

Rajat had been looking at the tapes of the video he had

accumulated over the last six months and he had noted something and wasn't happy about it.

'*I don't get it?* You son of a bitch. I just went through the security tapes and I saw what you did that day. You think you can keep your job by blackmailing me through that video? Not only will I kick you out from here, I will sue you and your friends' asses to hell. Believe me, man. I will fuck the happiness of everyone who knows you. Everyone. You think a stupid video can do something to me? Who will you show it to, Saurav? The police? What do you think they will do? You think after you show them the video, it won't leak out in the open? What if it does? What will happen to those very sweet girls, Saurav? Would you like their blood on your hands? Would you destroy their lives? So, what did you think, asshole? You can get through to me with that bloody video? Get this, not only will I eat your jobs, I will make sure that you don't get to anywhere in the entire damned industry.'

Saurav was sweating now. 'I w . . . will . . . will . . . go to the board,' he stammered, and wondered how twisted Thapar could be. He had never thought about doing anything with the video, let alone blackmail Thapar for personal gain. It was the last thing he would have done, but it was the first thing Thapar thought he would do.

'Aha! Very intelligent. What do you think? They are innocent? I have the security tapes, Saurav. *Everyone* is fucking the shit out of each other in the car park. Oh, am I forgetting something? Your very beloved sir, Deb, is smashing some very expensive car in one of them. I believe it was Sumita's. I am sure she is going to love it! I wonder if he now has that kind of money to pay her back for the damage he did to the car. A criminal case would do loads to his glittering career.'

'What do you want me to do?' Saurav asked, just wanting the conversation to be over.

'That is more like it. Here is the deal. Give me the video and sign an affidavit of an amount that even your father won't be able to pay, declaring that it is the only copy. Once you do that, I may give you your job.'

'And my friends retain their jobs?'

'Oh, no, no, no! Did I not tell you? I am calling the shots here. I can get away with not giving you anything. Remember, you cannot do anything with it.'

He was right. He couldn't. If he tried, he would ruin the lives of two very young women. He could not possibly have done that.

Remember, you cannot do anything with it
Remember, you cannot do anything with it.
Remember, you cannot do anything with it.

Saurav kept repeating these lines in his head, which was now heavy with the guilt of costing his friends their jobs. He cursed himself for acting smart that day and recording the video. Garima had asked him to stop but he hadn't listened.

'Sir . . .' he said.

'Seems like you have decided.'

'I wasn't . . . I wasn't going to give this to the police,' he stuttered. 'Or the board.'

'Good boy. You will keep your job. That is the kind of cooperation that I expect from my employees,' Thapar said.

'I always intended to give . . . give it to you,' he said, as he fumbled with words.

'Good for you. Good for you, Saurav.'

'Since you are so busy . . .' he said.

'Yes?' Thapar said.

'I was thinking of hand-delivering it to your home. Maybe your wife?'

There was silence. After a few seconds passed, Thapar said without any hint of worry, 'Go ahead. I . . . I . . . don't care. She is okay with all this.'

But it was too late. He was petrified. Thapar never took so long to respond and he NEVER stammered. Saurav knew that it was the only way out and he probed in further.

'Are you sure, Mr Thapar? This was what you said in the video. It's very clear and audible. *Oh, Chandni, you are so good, I can fuck you all day. If it weren't for my ugly wife, I would take you home.* And then you laughed, Mr Rajat Thapar.'

'That can't be,' he said. 'I couldn't have said that. You couldn't have recorded that.'

Saurav could tell Thapar was nervous, it was too evident in his voice.

'N96. It might not have the best speakers or alarm. But it has a great microphone.'

'So? What do you want, Saurav? What are you trying to say?'

'I am trying to say that it's time to re-negotiate. I get my job,' he said and patted himself for the turn of events. It was insane and he couldn't quite believe it happened.

'I don't care,' Rajat said.

'Okay, even I don't. Seems like your kids and your wife are going to love a forty-year-old dad who can make twenty-year-old girls scream in a parking lot! I don't think they would like you that much after that. I don't give a fuck about your job. Do whatever. But let me tell you, after I show this to your wife, you would be paying more than our combined worth in alimony. You want that, fine with me!'

'Saurav, do you have any idea who you are talking to?'

'Do *you* know who *you* are talking to? I'm from Delhi, you bastard. I can you get picked up from wherever I want to and no one will know where you disappeared,' Saurav said as his Delhi genes kicked in and he felt invincible.

'What do you want?' Thapar asked finally, after he saw that Saurav knew what he was doing. He backed down.

'That is more like it. I want my job back.'

'Done.'

'And my friends' jobs.'

'Done.'

'Super cool.'

'The video?' he asked meekly.

'Now that I am not signing any affidavit or anything, you won't ever be sure if there exists another copy or not. So, I think you would like to give that a skip.'

'The deal rides on it, Saurav.'

'Okay then. The deal is off. None of us was expecting to get our jobs anyway.'

'Fine! It is a deal,' he squeaked.

'And just one question. Is Sumita Bhasin leaving the company?'

'No. Why?'

'I hope you won't miss her, as you would have to throw her out.'

Saurav disconnected the phone at that and checked his phone. The video was there, but it was hidden. He clicked on *restore*. Garima had made him delete it, but he hadn't had the heart to and had hidden it. He found the Megha pictures in the hidden folder, too. He deleted them.

He came back to the living room and slipped in next to Riya.

'Who was it?'

'Nobody,' he said, as he hugged her.

'What did nobody say?' She kissed him as she pulled the quilt over both of them.

'Nobody said that all of us are very smart and we deserve to be happy.' He hugged her and they slept off.

32

The bell ran incessantly and Abhijeet was the first one to wake up. Abhijeet looked at his watch and it was six, and dragged his feet towards the door, his head felt heavy and his body tired. Till the time he opened the door and saw Shruti standing outside, he wasn't really aware of where he was.

'Shruti?' he asked, puzzled. 'Oh, Shruti, come. Where *were* you?' Abhijeet asked.

'Out,' Shruti replied. She had thought it would be hard for her to even bear the sight of any one of them, but she was surprisingly happy and she wanted to hug Abhijeet.

'Look we are very . . . sorry . . .' Abhijeet said and hugged her and she couldn't react.

'It's okay,' she said and hugged him tighter and they both had tears in their eyes.

'We were so worried! Where had you gone? And why did you resign? I mean why!'

'There was a reason, but it is okay! I am not worried now.'

'We were. We love you so much. I mean, we are really sorry. We had planned to make this day special for you and we waited but you didn't turn up.'

Shruti saw the lopsided charts, read the words on them and her eyes welled up.

'This is so sweet, this is so sweet!'

'It's nothing. We wish we could have done more!'

'You don't have to,' she said and they hugged again.

'I wish things hadn't gone so bad,' Abhijeet said.

'Leave it, Abhijeet. I want you to meet someone,' she said and pointed in Rishab's direction. At this, Rishab thrust out his hand to shake Abhijeet's. He had been standing there, witnessing the tearful reunion.

'Rishab,' he said.

'Abhijeet.'

'Heard a lot about you.'

'I hope she didn't bitch about me,' Abhijeet said. 'So? I have never heard about you. You guys are college friends?'

'We met yesterday.'

'What?' Abhijeet asked. 'Where? How? Like yesterday?'

'Nothing, really,' Shruti said, 'It is the usual stuff that happens when you meet someone in a club, you know. We met, we raced a jet, then we got on that jet, flew to Delhi, had lunch there and came back,' she said sarcastically.

'Are you drunk?'

'No, I am not. What makes you think I am?'

'If you don't want to tell, it is okay!' Abhijeet said.

'Abhijeet, I swear, my tone may not suggest it, but this is the truth,' she said and winked at Rishab, who smiled shyly.

'Why are you doing this to me?'

'We are doing nothing,' Shruti said. She was still smiling and clutching at Rishab's arm.

'Rishab, what is going on here?'

'She is not lying,' Rishab said.

'You raced a jet. That is what you want me to believe, Rishab?' he asked and stopped. 'Wait! This can't be him. *Rishab?* You look familiar . . .' His mouth fell open. 'Rishab what?'

'*What* as in?' Shruti asked.

'Surname, damn it?' Abhijeet asked.

'Manchanda,' Rishab said.

'*Rishab Manchanda*?' Abhijeet asked disbelievingly. '*The* Rishab Manchanda? You're THE Rishab Manchanda?'

'I guess so, yes,' he said.

'You guys know each other?' Shruti asked, surprised at Abhijeet's behaviour and still acting as if she didn't know that Rishab was actually Rishab *Manchanda*.

'I know him,' he said.

'How?' Shruti asked.

'The whole country knows him, Shruti! Are you blind? Manchanda Petroleum? Manchanda Textiles? Manchanda Telecom? Are you out of your mind?'

'What? Wait? Are you? Oh shit! You are! Are you? Oh no! You are Rishab? Manchanda? You are really?' Shruti kept repeating things, acting surprised.

'Now, this is embarrassing,' Rishab conceded.

'Why didn't you tell me?' Shruti asked.

'You didn't ask,' he said. 'And I didn't think it was important enough to tell.'

'Oh my God! Shit, shit, shit.' She held her head in her hands.

The commotion got the rest three of them up, who were buried in the blankets till then.

'Abhijeet?' Garima said groggily, eyes still closed, while Saurav and Riya were staring goggle-eyed at Rishab. 'I had a strange dream . . . that Shruti was home . . . and Rishab Manchanda . . . you know him, right? That super-hot guy from *Business World*? He is here . . . strange dream, no?'

'Garima, get up,' Abhijeet said.

'In a while,' she said, as Saurav continued to stare at Rishab who shifted in his place in embarrassment. He felt like a zoo animal.

'For a minute, please Garima, wake up.'

Garima woke up and saw Rishab and Shruti standing hand in hand and she felt her mouth drop to the floor. 'Oh my God! What on earth is he doing here? Is he really him? Are you? What? Why?' She threw the blanket aside and got up on her knees and opened her eyes.

'Yes, he is Rishab Manchanda,' Abhijeet said.

'Saurav?' Riya looked at Saurav.

'Yes, Riya?'

'Is this Rishab Manchanda? Really?' Riya asked. She turned to Rishab who smiled, 'I love you so much! I mean, you came on the cover of *Business World* and I loved your suit!'

'Riya?' Saurav said.

'Yes?'

'Shut up,' he said, as he put his hand across her mouth painfully.

They both waved from where they were sitting. They stared and smiled stupidly at Rishab. After everyone had done his or her bit of getting surprised and staring, everyone hugged each other and looked at Rishab as if he was a lab experiment. Everyone hugged Shruti and they told her how sorry they were, tears rolled down, more apologies were exchanged and God was thanked for everything. Everyone was sorry and everyone cried their hearts out. They told each other how they would always be there for each other and how their lives were incomplete without each other. Garima and Shruti found it hard to keep the flow of tears in check. After a good half hour, things crawled back to normalcy.

'So, what's the story?' Saurav asked Rishab and Shruti, who were sitting hand in hand in a corner.

And then Shruti started to narrate every moment of what happened to four enraptured listeners, who alternated between looking at her and a red-faced Rishab. She skipped the last part of their meeting and left them to guess what must have happened.

'Did it really not strike you?' Abhijeet asked what Saurav had already asked a million times during Shruti's narration.

'No, it didn't. One more time you ask that, and I will kick you,' Shruti said. 'I had other things on my mind and I thought there could be other guys with the same name.'

'Okay. And yes, now that the big shock is over, I have something to tell you guys,' Saurav said.

'What?' Abhijeet asked, as all eyes turned to him.

'Thapar called,' Saurav said and paused dramatically. Their

hearts skipped a beat. 'The video. He knew about it. He saw me making the video.'

'What? How? I knew something was going to go wrong. I told you, Saurav! It was a bad idea. We are screwed,' Garima panicked.

'What did he say?' Abhijeet asked, as he tried to calm Garima.

'Turns out Rajat is quite a pussy in front of his wife.'

'Come to the point, Saurav,' Garima said irritably.

'The point is, he kind of tried to freak me out, but when I said that I would give it to his wife, he kind of pissed in his pants and gave us our jobs back and promised he would fire Sumita. That is it, in very short words. Fine? Man, you just killed the suspense out of it,' he said, visibly pissed at Garima.

'*Are you serious?*' Abhijeet asked.

'Do I look like I am laughing?'

'What exactly happened?' Garima asked, still not believing what he'd just said.

'What crap? First, you tell me to come to the point. So, I told you. That is what happened! We all have our jobs. Shruti, too!'

After that, they all shouted and danced and hugged, as Rishab watched on.

33

'I am so happy for you,' Garima said to Shruti, as they both entered the kitchen to make something for the guys. Saurav was hungry again.

'Thank you.'

'I am so glad that things are back to what they were like before.'

'They are better now,' Shruti said.

'Yes, better. It is unbelievable, isn't it? Of all people, you met Rishab Manchanda? What are the odds of that!'

'Don't tell anyone but I almost knew who he was the moment I first saw him walk up to me in the nightclub last night,' Shruti said. 'I knew he was Rishab Manchanda. You have no idea how much I wanted to tell him that I knew who he was but I stayed shut. I didn't want to gush all over him and lose him.'

She looked at Garima and said, 'Now that is luck, isn't it? Life is fair, after all. Now all you have to do is to hang on to him and not let him go!'

'You can count on that,' she said and winked and they laughed.

'So, a rich guy, huh?' Garima said and smiled.

'I just got lucky,' she said and smiled back.

Meanwhile, Saurav and Abhijeet drove to the nearest market to get a list of things Garima and Shruti had asked them to buy.

'It is so cool that we can be together now,' Saurav said.

'I know.'

'You owe me a *thank you*, man! I know I would have proved to be a major reason had you been kicked out. But still, you weren't!' Saurav said.

'Thanks, man. But it wouldn't have been too bad to lose the job either,' Abhijeet responded. 'Because now I have Garima and she said I could work with her dad if I wanted to. That would be cool, wouldn't it? Managing an entire business all by myself and stuff?'

'But, she does have a brother, right?'

'No. She doesn't! How could you not know that? It is all hers. She is the only child, so it's only the two of us who has to take the business forward.'

'What a turn of events!'

'Isn't it?' Abhijeet smiled. 'My rich girlfriend.'

Epilogue

And the year passed and Silverman got back to its feet. It was bought by a gigantic cash-rich investment bank in Japan. Dinesh and Sameer are doing well for themselves.

Shruti left the company and moved to Mumbai with Rishab. They fly down to Hyderabad often. For lunch, dinner or brunch. Shruti now has a flying licence. She paid off her father's debt. They don't talk now, no matter how much they call her.

Saurav is still working in Silverman Finance. Riya joined Silverman, too, when she passed out of Shri Ram College of Commerce. Rajat and Saurav have never talked after that day, except once. Riya was the only person Silverman hired that year and it is no surprise how she got there.

Saurav sold his car after Rishab gifted him his Porsche. He weighs only eighty kilograms now.

Garima and Abhijeet are still together. They are very much in love. They are moving to Delhi next month. Garima's parents really like Abhijeet and want him to help them run the business.

I met these guys last at Shruti's engagement. It was a glamorous do where film stars were the order of the day. Shruti was looking gorgeous in her blazing blue glittery saree that Riya chose for her.

I caught her alone for a moment and we hugged. She'd never

looked happier. When you are down three glasses of champagne, you have a constant smile plastered on your face.

~

'Fairytale, eh? And sure, you look like a princess! Awesome. I have always had the hots for you,' I said.

'Thanks,' she said in slurred words.

'No, you are looking ravishing! And isn't this nice? He came along just as you lost everything. I still find it hard to believe.'

'Love is a strange thing,' she said, a little lost, a little drunk from all the expensive champagne.

'It sure is. How much time has it been? A year? Does he still love you as much?'

'It's been two years, not one. Two years since I talked to Sachin . . . don't know . . . who knows where he is . . .'

'I was talking about *Rishab*.'

'Him? Oh, him? Yes, he loves me. Of course I love him, too.' She laughed out and added. 'Till I find someone better.'

We both laughed out. That last line sounded vaguely familiar. The smile faded away quite quickly from her face as she gulped her drink and looked me.

'Love can wait,' she said and looked at me before finally smiling at me and added, 'Diamonds cannot.'

She walked away, looking at her six-carat diamond ring.

If It's Not Forever
It's Not Love

Durjoy Datta • Nikita Singh

To the everlasting power of love . . .

When Deb, an author and publisher, survives the bomb blasts at Chandni Chowk, he knows his life is nothing short of a miracle. And though he escapes with minor injuries, he is haunted by the images and voices that he heard on that unfortunate day.

Even as he recovers, his feet take him to where the blasts took place. From the burnt remains he discovers a diary. It seems to belong to a dead man who was deeply in love with a girl. As he reads the heartbreaking narrative, he knows that this story must never be left incomplete. Thus begins Deb's journey with his girlfriend, Avantika, and his best friend, Shrey, to hand over the diary to the man's beloved.

Deeply engrossing and powerfully told, *If It's Not Forever . . .* tells an unforgettable tale of love and life.